"You should at least have one last fling before settling down."

"A fling?" she repeated suspiciously. "I don't have flings."

"What? Never?"

"You mean like a one-night stand with a complete stranger? No. No way."

"Not a one-night stand with a stranger. Just a fling with someone you're attracted to—without attaching forever after, babies and a fiftieth wedding anniversary to the package."

Her eyes narrowed. "Can't I have a fling with someone I'm attracted to—and attach the whole package, too?"

"Sure. If you find one."

"Good. Let's just work on that, then."

"Okay. You're the boss. But I still think a fling is just what you need."

Interesting suggestion, Tom, his conscience taunted. And just who did you have in mind for her "last fling"?

Shut up, he told himself.

Dear Reader,

We're constantly striving to bring you the best romance fiction by the most exciting authors…and in Harlequin Romance® we're especially keen to feature fresh, sparkling, warmly emotional novels. Modern love stories to suit your every mood: poignant, deeply moving stories; lively, upbeat romances with sparks flying; or sophisticated, edgy novels with an international flavor.

All our authors are special, and we hope you continue to enjoy each month's new selection of Harlequin Romance® novels. This month, we're delighted to feature another story in our TANGO miniseries. *Mission: Marriage* by Hannah Bernard fizzes with energy, warmth and wit, and is Hannah's third book!

We hope you enjoy this book by Hannah Bernard— and look out for future sparkling stories in Harlequin Romance®. If you'd like to share your thoughts and comments with us, do please write to:

The Harlequin Romance Editors
Harlequin Mills & Boon Ltd.
Eton House (or e-mail Tango@hmb.co.uk)
18-24 Paradise Road
Richmond
Surrey TW9 1SR
U.K.

Happy reading!

The Editors

MISSION: MARRIAGE
Hannah Bernard

TANGO
IT TAKES TWO...

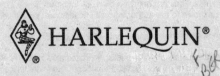

HARLEQUIN®

TORONTO • NEW YORK • LONDON
AMSTERDAM • PARIS • SYDNEY • HAMBURG
STOCKHOLM • ATHENS • TOKYO • MILAN • MADRID
PRAGUE • WARSAW • BUDAPEST • AUCKLAND

ISBN 0-373-03792-9

MISSION: MARRIAGE

First North American Publication 2004.

Copyright © 2003 by Hannah Bernard.

This edition published by arrangement with Harlequin Books S.A.

® and TM are trademarks of the publisher. Trademarks indicated with ® are registered in the United States Patent and Trademark Office, the Canadian Trade Marks Office and in other countries.

Visit us at www.eHarlequin.com

Printed in U.S.A.

CHAPTER ONE

BABIES are obnoxious, Lea decided, balancing her friend's eleven-month-old on her lap. Yes. Totally obnoxious. Not only did bringing them into this world involve hours—if not nine months—of suffering, but once they were there, they were loud, filthy, demanding, and never gave a moment's peace from cleaning and feeding and everything else that needed to be done. They consumed their parents' lives, swallowed them up whole, leaving no time or energy for anything else. Then they grew up to be sullen, ungrateful, troublesome teenagers, who after years of turning their parents' hair gray, finally became adults, left the nest, and never bothered to call or visit with their own little brats.

Yes. Babies were obnoxious.

And, God, how she wanted one.

Unexpected moisture in her eyes blurred the sight of obnoxious little Danny, and the bowl of food she was currently try to get on the inside of him. What was wrong with her? She ripped a tissue out of her purse and managed to get rid of the tears under the pretext of cleaning some of the mashed bananas from the tip of Danny's snubby little nose.

"Everything okay?" Anne chirped from where she was loading the fridge with groceries.

"Why shouldn't everything be okay?" Lea snapped back, nerves suddenly too fragile to deal with her friend's inquisitions. Anne raised an eyebrow in surprise.

"Danny isn't always fond of bananas," she said. "Sometimes he spits everything out. I was just wondering if he was behaving."

Lea shook her head. "Sorry, I didn't mean to snap at you. Yeah, he's eating." Eating was one way of putting it. The mashed banana was on his face, in his downy black hair, on his chest—not to mention all over her own shirt—but she did believe some of it had made it into his mouth. From there, some of it had probably followed the standard path down to his stomach, but percentage wise, it wasn't a lot of the original product. She added another negative thing to her I'm-better-off-without-a-baby list: inefficient eating habits.

"He tends to eat more when strangers feed him, actually," Anne said. "Gives him something to think about other than finding new ways to make us tear our hair out in frustration."

Lea tilted another spoonful of banana into Danny's mouth and watched half of it slide down his chin and drop onto his colorful terry bib. The child slapped the glob with his fist, splashing some on the wall and on Lea's face. For a moment she wondered about the status of the floor, but decided not to look down. Ignorance really was bliss. "He's a lot of work, isn't he?"

"Endless," Anne sighed with a smile and plopped down in a chair on the other side of the table. "And will be even more work once he's moving around on his own. But he's sleeping through the night now, did I tell you?" Excitement made her nearly bounce in her seat. "Last Saturday night was the first night in a whole year that I got whole seven hours of uninterrupted sleep. I couldn't believe it when he finally woke me up and I saw what time it was."

"Yes, I know, you told me." Anne had called at seven o'clock on Sunday morning with this exciting news, nearly incoherent with exhilaration—or maybe it was sleep overdose. She'd woken Lea up, who in her sleepy state had committed the nearly unforgivable crime of failing to register the importance of this event. Another vote against babies: lack of sleep at night, no weekend lie-ins. For *years*.

Yup. Better off without one. Definitely. *Are you listening, biological clock?*

"I'm sorry," Anne laughed, looking embarrassed. "The universe shrinks after you have a baby and are staying at home. Suddenly the tiny everyday miracles are such a big deal, and you automatically assume everyone else is interested in them." She smiled wryly. "You also tend to assume the rest of the world gets up at six o'clock, weekend or not."

"I'm interested," Lea protested. "And it was fine. I shouldn't waste my weekends sleeping away the mornings, anyway."

"You can put Danny in the chair, if you like. You'd get less food on you that way."

"It's okay. I like holding him."

In fact, she didn't want to let go. When she'd picked up Danny this afternoon, she'd suddenly identified the stark feeling of emptiness that had invaded her life recently.

She wanted a baby. She *needed* a baby.

It made no sense. She wasn't married, didn't even have a boyfriend, had a busy and fulfilling career, and no reason in the world to want a baby in her life at this time.

Yet she did. Nature was making her wishes clear. Logic didn't stand a chance against the devious lady, who'd obviously been counting up the years, tallying each of the wasted eggs that vanished one by one each month.

The intensity of the longing was almost frightening. She must have hit the snooze button on her biological clock one time too many. It was now ringing with a vengeance.

It was that birthday, she thought with a silent sigh. The dreaded, looming thirtieth birthday was approaching rapidly with all its connotations. Add to that the gruesome fact that this week also happened to mark one year since she'd kicked Harry out of her life. Her Prince Charming who'd turned out to be the biggest toad of all. She'd wasted years on Mr. Wrong, and what did she have to show for it? Yup, a distrust of human nature and a bottomed-out self-esteem. Not to mention a butchered CD collection.

But her year of wallowing in self-pity, nursing her broken heart, was up. It was time to move on. Meet new people.

Meet new men.

If only she could figure out the basics. How did one even go about meeting men these days? Meeting the *right* men? They certainly weren't showing up out of the blue.

"So, are you seeing anyone?"

Anne the mind reader. Lea shrugged. "No one special." She didn't know what it was, a matter of pride or dignity, perhaps, but she felt uncomfortable, sharing her feelings with her settled friends, who had their future all figured out with their husbands and their babies. It felt awkward.

"No one at all, isn't it?"

Lea shrugged again. "I've been busy."

"It's been forever since you broke up with the rat. Isn't it about time you started dating again?" Now her friend's voice was reproachful. Not a first, either. Emancipation be damned, apparently it was still the single woman's sacred duty to keep husband-hunting until she found one.

Danny snuggled up to her and yawned.

Husbands did have their advantages. She wouldn't be getting an obnoxious brat of her own without one, would she?

But the very words "start dating" sent shivers down her back. "Again? What do you mean *again?* I met Harry my first week in college. Unless you count high school, I've never dated in my life."

"Well, it can't be that difficult. Everybody's doing it."

Lea shook her head. "I'd screw it up. Have you read the women's magazines lately? They're writing ten-page articles just on the anatomy of first kisses, let alone anything…." She covered Danny's ears, just in case what she was about to say would warp him for life. "I glanced at one article at the dentist's last week. There are *rules* for what kind of things you can do with a guy your first time together. Can you believe it? You can't do *this*, unless he does *that*, and then only if you've done *this* previously…" She groaned and allowed Danny to twist his head out of her grasp. He waved his fists around, then settled down to sucking his thumb, grumbling quietly to himself, no doubt about the injustice of having been cut off from this educational conversation.

"Rules? Really?" Anne looked fascinated. "I haven't read those magazines for ages. What kind of things can't you do unless he does what? Who made up those rules? How do you even know they're for real? How can you be sure the guy knows about them? What happens if one of you breaks them?''

Lea refused to grin at her friend's teasing, and took her questions at face value instead. ''I don't know. I barely glanced at the headlines.''

''Did it come with some kind of a flowchart? You know, something like 'If male does A, do B, else C, unless he does D, in which case go straight to XXX'? Or maybe a checklist to put in your bedside drawer?''

''I don't know,'' Lea repeated, feeling grumpy. This wasn't funny. Well, maybe it was funny to people to whom it wasn't relevant, but it was deadly serious to her, who might have to deal with these situations. ''I wasn't interested.''

''You don't have to be interested. Look at it as homework for dating school.''

Lea rested her head on top of Danny's head. ''I don't want to learn. It's scary. Somehow dating has evolved into this intricate game with all kinds of subtle rules and scripts.'' She shuddered. ''Just thinking about it frightens the hell out of me.''

''Well, if you want to meet guys, you'll have to,'' Anne said rationally. ''Mr. Rights don't show up on their own. You have to go find them.'' She snapped her fingers. ''Tell you what, I'll ask Brian if there isn't someone at work we can set you up with. He works with literally hundreds of guys, after all—there has to be one there for you.''

''No!'' Oh, God no, not a blind date. ''Anne, I'm not ready. I haven't even read the first-kiss articles! I'll have to do some serious research before I dive in.''

''You'll never be 'ready,' Lea. It doesn't work that way. You just have to do it. Why not give it a chance?

One date won't kill you." She smiled and held her hands out for her child. Danny squealed with pleasure, squirming to push himself into his mother's arms.

Lea felt bereft, her arms empty without the child.

"One date?" Anne pushed. "Just to get your toes wet. Look at it as practice."

Lea began to shake her head, but Danny chose that exact moment to look up at his mother and laugh, then wrapped his arms around her neck and gave her a wet, banana kiss on her chin. Lea felt her heart liquefy and head straight for her ovaries with instructions to prepare for immediate procreation.

If she were planned on ever having children, a man was kind of a necessary evil in the whole process, not only making the child, but caring for it. Being a single mother was not something she had a desire for. A child needed two parents.

Anne was right. It was time. It wasn't about just grabbing anyone for procreation, but if she had hopes for a future with a family, now was the time to start looking. Who knew how many years that would take? She didn't have all the time in the world any more. It was time to test the waters.

"Okay," she conceded. "Just as a practice date. But you better pick someone…not dreadful."

Anne hesitated. "What's your definition of dreadful?"

Uh, oh.

Could this be any worse?

Lea groaned under her breath as her date tried for another footsie. She sat up straighter and tucked her feet under her chair. It hadn't looked too bad at first, not compared to some of the blind dates horror stories she'd read. James was presentable, didn't pick his nose over the appetizer, and was even a semi-interesting conversationalist, even though his topics of choice all seemed rather similar.

But that was it, as far as the good side went.

For one, he yelled at the waiters and waitresses. Not even in an impolite way—yet—but just as a routine way of getting their attention, his shrill voice echoing from the dark wooden walls of the cozy restaurant. Lea had nearly jumped out of her too-tight heels the first time. The second time, when every single eye in the restaurant had turned on them, a couple of people out of eyeshot even standing up to check what the ruckus was all about, she'd almost slid all the way under the table in an effort to pretend she wasn't with that man. Her foot had accidentally brushed his—which was when the footsie had started.

Things had gone downhill from there, and they weren't even halfway through the appetizer yet. Thank God for cocktails.

Anne and Brian would be hearing about this for a long, long time, Lea thought grimly.

There was another couple just two tables away, also on their first date, judging from the snatches of conversation that drifted over. They too were making their way through the appetizer. As James called the waiter over for the fourth time, Lea occupied herself by concentrating on the other couple. The guy was probably in his early thirties, and didn't yell at the waiters, which currently made him a dream date in her book. Not that his looks hurt any either. The woman was several years younger, her hair long and blond, her laughter loud, and she seemed to have a black belt in flirting.

The blonde obviously knew all the rules, all the in

and outs of this mysterious dating culture, Lea thought enviously. She should be taking notes. The show was fascinating. Flip hair, lean forward, show cleavage, tilt head sideways and smile coyly.

Hmm. Only, it didn't seem to be working. The guy leaned back and seemed rather bored, although his smile was polite enough. He picked up his fork and speared his shrimp, his attention wandering to James who was waving the menu in front of the waiter.

The blonde made another attempt to draw her date's attention with the flip hair, coy smile routine. The man seemed to realize what was expected of him. He put his fork down, leaned forward and talked for a bit, seemingly answering a question.

Meanwhile, his date was scouting the restaurant, and then stood up, and headed for the rest room.

Maybe she should follow the blonde to the rest room for some girl talk. That girl looked like she knew a thing or two. She could drill her about all the details that were nagging at her. Like, was she expected to kiss her date tonight? Would she be breaking all the rules if she didn't? Would James charge her with violations of dating ethics if she made do with a handshake and then escaped into her apartment?

She glanced at her date and decided she really, really didn't want to kiss him if there was any way out of it.

He was bashing the poor waiter again, but at least that activity was distracting him from the footsie game. Apparently there was a typo on the menu. His monologue was drawing more and more attention from the neighboring tables, not the least from the blonde's date, who was looking at her with certain sympathy in his gaze and a weak smile pulling at one corner of his mouth.

Oh, Lord. Not only was she on her first date since high school, she had strangers pitying her.

Blind date, she mouthed at the stranger on an impulse, shrugging helplessly.

The man raised his eyebrows, then grimaced. *Me too,* he mouthed back, sending her a sympathetic grin and a rueful shake of his head.

That one, she might not mind kissing at the end of the evening, she conceded. Gorgeous eyes—dark blue, from what she could tell from here—and the smile was even better. The blonde had nothing to complain about. Some girls had all the luck.

The third waiter incident was over at last. Lea tried to catch the waiter's eye for an apologetic look, but the harassed young man was hurrying away from the table, and she didn't blame him. Worse, James's toes were digging into her foot again. She pulled her legs under the chair once more, but he seemed to consider that a coy game of playing hard to get, and his foot was now on her calf.

What the hell was he thinking?

Once again she cursed her inexperience at this thing. Was this a normal part of whatever activities were involved in a first date in today's world, or would she be justified in being insulted enough to throw down her napkin and stalk out of the restaurant?

She didn't want to make a scene. She hated making scenes but that man wasn't taking a hint, was he?

She'd try an unsubtle one.

"I'm sorry, but your foot keeps bumping into me," she said with a polite laugh, once again moving her legs. "Not a lot of room under these tables, is there?"

Doggone it, it worked. James's face froze in astonished shock, then his feet were mercifully withdrawn.

So was conversation. So were smiles.

Which only left arguments with the waiter, didn't it?

Lea groaned under her breath after making several attempts to start a conversation, all met with an icy yes, no, or noncommittal grunts if she asked open-ended questions.

What a guy.

She gave up for the time being, and instead went for another glass of wine. She picked at the smoked salmon, but there was no way anything could have a taste in these circumstances. This was dreadful. If she clicked her heels three times, would she be transported out of here? Anywhere, any time, would be better than right here, right now. She was being ignored by her date, who'd obviously been insulted by her refusal to be toe-groped under the table. For all she knew, she was being terribly unfair. Maybe there was even something she should be doing in return. Like scratching behind his ears with her fork.

She might as well have stepped onto another planet.

Their next-table neighbors weren't doing much better, although she could see under their table and at least the blue-eyed guy didn't seem to belong to the Footsie Cult. He seemed, however, to have lost his appetite and was leaning back in his seat, looking with a bit of a terror at the blonde, who had finished her appetizer and was now blowing green bubble gum bubbles in between her energetic chatting. Her voice was loud, and her favorite subject matter seemed to be celebrity gossip. Then she stuck her gum on her plate and jumped to her feet, heading for the rest room for the second time in twenty minutes.

Mr. Blue Eyes slumped in relief and took a deep breath, rubbing his face with both hands. He then picked up his fork and started pushing his food around his plate. He met Lea's gaze again, and they sighed silently in unison.

James started hollering for the waiter again, and Lea stood up so quickly that the heavy wooden chair almost toppled. "I'll just…" she waved a hand in the direction of the rest room. "I'll be right back…" she murmured. She'd probably be able to hear the one-sided argument in there. Hopefully she could just stay locked in there until everything was silent again.

"Darling…I'm sorry. So sorry."

Lea almost flew up the wall in shock. The blue-eyed stranger was all of a sudden at her side, his hand on her shoulder, intense regret in his voice, She nearly panicked. Two psychos in one night, what were the odds?

Then she noticed him winking at her.

"Can you forgive me?" he continued, the look in his eyes beseeching, and behind the playacting, a wicked glint of humor. And they *were* blue. Very blue, she noticed vaguely, before she was distracted by a warm kiss pressed to the back of her hand. "I've missed you so much, darling," he said, his voice low and intimate, but just loud enough to make sure James would hear. "I've been going out of my mind. When I saw you again, I knew we'd been so wrong to break up."

Lea hesitated, her mind racing to keep up with the sudden galloping of her heart. What's a girl to do?

She glanced once at Mr. Footsie and made up her mind. Sometimes, the devil you didn't know was the better choice. "I'm sorry too," she said, throwing her arms around the stranger's neck. "It was a such a mistake," she mumbled into his chest, feeling exhilarated by her uncharacteristic behavior. The man's arms came around her in a tight hug and she felt his breath against her hair as her nose squashed against his shoulder.

Oh, wow. This was interesting. No wonder people went out on dates if this sort of thing happened to them on a regular basis.

"What's going on?" a familiar whiny voice demanded. Lea pulled away from the stranger, who kept his arm around her shoulders, and tried to look contrite and deliriously happy at the same time. Good thing she'd taken those acting lessons back in high school, but then again, the prospect of escaping Mr. Footsie the Sulk was indeed occasion for delirious happiness. That last glass of wine hadn't hurt either.

"I'm sorry, James, but this is my…fiancé," she told him. "We recently broke up…but…" she tightened her hold of her savior's arm and smiled up at him. "It was a mistake. We belong together."

The blonde, back from the rest room, joined them, looking furious at seeing her date with another woman in his arms. "What the hell is going on? Who's that?"

"I'm sorry, Beth," he said. "I'm in love with her. I always was. I thought we were over, but when I saw her again…" The stranger smiled down at Lea, and once again the look in his eyes was so loving and passionate that she was almost fooled herself.

He was *good*.

"Beth…" He looked at the blonde. "I'm sorry. I thought I was ready to date again, but when I saw her again, I just knew…I'm sorry to cut our date so short. Can you understand?"

"Of course. It's okay," the blonde said, her eyes widening. "Oh, this is so romantic…I'm so happy for you." Lea was astonished to see tears fill the blonde's eyes. "So romantic," she sniffed. "Just like on *Rendezvous with Romance.* I haven't missed an episode since I was sixteen. This could be Pierre and Paradise, realizing they're still in love despite everything." She jumped at them, wrapping one arm around each of their necks, giving Lea a constructive lesson in perfumes-to-wear-on-first-dates. "Congratulations."

"Thank you, Beth." Blue Eyes kissed the blonde on the cheek. "Thank you for being so understanding."

Lea sneaked a peek at James. She imagined he wouldn't be quite so understanding. More likely that he was on the verge of another tantrum.

James's jaw was working, his face flushed in anger, but he seemed to be working on a way to save his wounded pride. He stared at Beth for a while and took a deep breath, collecting his dignity. Then he stood up, gave a small bow and gestured toward Lea's abandoned chair, ignoring Lea and Blue Eyes completely. "Why don't you join me?" he offered. "It looks like we're both getting dumped, so we might as well finish our meals together, don't you think?"

Beth's cherubic face lit up and she wasted no time in claiming her seat. "Absolutely. Thank you!"

Lea stuttered some hurried goodbyes as her savior insisting on leaving money on the table to pay for all four meals, then put his arm over her shoulder and pulled her toward the exit. She made a mental note of remembering to pay him back, but then everything was drowned in cheerful applause from every corner of the restaurant. Blue Eyes turned around and bowed, his arm still tight around her. Lea felt her face catch fire. She glanced up at him, and he grinned back. Was this something he did every day? All in a dating day's work?

She waved weakly to their audience, shrugged his arm from her shoulder and grabbed his hand. She'd do the leading. She wanted out of here. *Now.*

Her motives for the sudden escape got the predictable interpretation, and laughter and a few wolf whistles slid through the door as it closed behind them.

What an evening.

This was it. Hand kisses from hunky strangers or not—dating was definitely not for her. Too risky. Too dangerous. Too unsettling.

She glanced sideways to the man holding her hand. Too...exciting?

"Wow," she breathed as soon as they had turned the corner and were out of sight of the restaurant windows. She stopped, almost stumbling on her heels, and glanced back toward the restaurant, relieved despite everything. She wouldn't have to go through the rest of the evening. The kissing dilemma had mercifully vanished. "Did that really happen, or am I having a very surreal dream?"

"It happened, believe it or not." The stranger grinned as he released her hand. "We're off the hook. Thank you for the rescue."

"Thank *you*." She shuddered. "What was happening to me was infinitely worse than green bubble gum."

He nodded. "Yeah. I noticed the cat and mouse game under the table. Not exactly a gentleman, is he?"

Lea shrugged. "You tell me. That's not a part of the regular dating ritual?"

The man frowned in confusion. "Ritual? Uh, no. Not that I know of, anyway."

"I don't do this a lot, you see. It's good to hear that's

not the standard. He... Oh! Poor Beth!" Lea groaned. "No, we can't do this. We can't leave her like this."

"Don't worry about Beth. She's a bit of a man-eater. A sentimental, cries at the drop of a hat, man-eater. If that guy goes out of line, he's likely to find himself with a lapful of gravy." He held out a hand. "I'm Thomas Carlisle."

"Lea Rhodes."

Thomas smiled. "Nice to meet you. Can I call you a taxi? Walk you to your car? Give you a ride home?"

"Taxi would be good. I just want to get home, curl up with my cat and cry my mascara off."

"Was it that bad?"

"I believe I've got the imprint of his toes on my ankle."

He winced. "Ouch. My sympathies. Some guys have no class."

"Dating sucks," she muttered. "And I'm no good at it."

"It's an art form," he agreed. "An acquired skill, definitely. Acquired taste, too. Not for everybody."

"You sound like an expert."

He grinned. "Yeah, well, when you're not interested in wedding bells and not looking to settle down, you get an extended run at the dating part. As they say, practice makes perfect, doesn't it?"

"Practice makes perfect?" She stared at him, wheels struggling to churn in her head. She wasn't drunk yet—but after a cocktail and two glasses of Chardonnay on an empty stomach she was damn close.

Practice? Hmm... Here she had run into someone not interested in commitment, just in casual dating. A serial dater. Someone with plenty of experience in this, someone who knew all about *what, when* and *how* when it came to the dating game.

He was right. He was perfect.

CHAPTER TWO

HE'D rescued the cutest damsel in distress from her own dragon's claws—a creep who thought he could grope his way to a woman's heart. He wasn't sure why his intervention had been needed—why the lady hadn't simply thrown her drink in the guy's face and fled the restaurant.

He wasn't sure either what had possessed him to stage such an elaborate play to rescue her. That hadn't been a part of the deal. He was just supposed to call Anne on his cell phone and she'd handle the rest— probably phone Lea and stage a fake emergency to get her out of there.

But something—he wasn't sure if it was the tedi-ousness of his own blind date, or the fascinating twin-kle in Lea's eyes when they'd communicated silently across the room in their parallel dilemmas—had com-pelled him to intervene.

And here they were, and he wasn't sure what to do now. Anne had threatened bodily harm if he let Lea know she'd gotten a stranger to chaperone her date. *Observe,* she'd instructed him. *Lea's not used to dating, and you know what blind dates can be like. If she runs into trouble, call me, and I'll take it from there.*

She'd left out the fact that her "spinster" friend was someone she really should have introduced him to a long time ago. Lovely dark hair and expressive green eyes that he'd seen radiate all sorts of emotion in the half-hour he'd been watching her at the restaurant.

Maybe he could turn this around to his advantage, he mused.

Yeah. Why not? He'd see if they could continue this date somewhere else.

He'd opened his mouth to say something when the look in Lea's eyes stopped him. The gratitude in her eyes didn't really surprise him, considering the action he'd witnessed under their table, but it had quickly been replaced with another expression. He tried smiling at her, and her eyes narrowed in a calculating look.

He forgot all about his plans for an impromptu date, and found himself wanting to take a step back.

Why was she all of a sudden looking at him much like he imagined the big bad wolf had looked at Little Red Riding Hood?

"Practice makes perfect, you say?" she said slowly, her cheeks still red from the excitement of the last few minutes—and perhaps from one drink too many. Then her voice rose in exhilaration. "This is terrific. You're just what I need. Finally fate decides to be on my side. It's about time, too."

"I'm just what you need?" Thomas asked.

"Yes!"

"And what is it that you *need?*" Judging by the wild look in her eyes, he wasn't sure he wanted to know, but it was probably safer to ask, before she went right ahead and helped herself to...whatever she needed.

"A guy like you. You know. A serial dater. A playboy."

"A *playboy?*" Thomas gave in to his instincts and took that cautious step back. Magical green eyes or not, had he rescued a slightly nuts—as well as tipsy—damsel in distress? "I'm definitely not a 'playboy.' I'm not even sure they make those outside of Hollywood."

She shrugged. "Okay, a playboy probably isn't the right word. I don't have the terminology quite straight. I took a crash course online last night. Amazing, the things you'll learn if you type 'dating' into a search engine. A *player,* that's what you're called, isn't it?"

"Huh?"

"Players," she repeated patiently. "Single men, playing the field for all it's worth, you're called players, aren't you?"

"Uh…I don't know. We are? They are?"

She didn't seem to have heard him, and she still had the big bad wolf look on her face. "Listen…" she said slowly. "We missed out on the main course and I don't think either of us ate much of our appetizer. I'm sure you're as hungry as I am. Can I buy you dinner somewhere? There's something I'd like to discuss with you." She hesitated. "I'm sorry—I'm sounding a bit crazy, aren't I?"

Thomas laughed, feeling a bit relieved. Nuts usually didn't realize they were sounding nuts. There might be an explanation for her weird ramblings. She might even be okay after all, which would be a definite plus to the evening since the damsel intrigued him a whole lot more than Beth had. "I won't deny that the thought crossed my mind."

"Sorry. But I have a problem, and I think you could help me solve it…" She paused and looked around. "There is a point to this, I promise. But it's a bit of a long story. What do you say about dinner? We need to eat anyway."

"Sounds great," he said. "And I really am starving. You don't stick gum on your plate, do you?"

She had a great smile, one that hadn't been much in evidence during her date with the footsie guy, except in her silent exchanges with *him.* "I promise. My chewing gum doesn't come in that shade of green, either." She glanced around again. "Where can we eat? Do you know this neighborhood?"

"Not really. But I think I know of a place that might have tables available. My car is here, we could drive there. It's maybe fifteen minutes away." He hesitated, realizing they were complete strangers. "On second thoughts, you probably prefer that we take a taxi, don't you?"

"Your car is fine," she said, which annoyed him. She should know better than to get into a car with someone she'd never met before, and here she was, walking with him toward the darkened parking lot without any qualms at all. He wasn't a psycho, but she didn't know that, did she? She shouldn't trust him at all.

But it was none of his business, was it? Wouldn't hurt to mention it to her later tonight, though. Or tell Anne to warn her friend not to be so trusting of strangers.

"You're sure Beth will be okay?" she asked, while fastening her seat belt. "I'm still feeling guilty about leaving them together."

"I'm positive. I never met her before tonight, but I've heard stories about her for a while. She won't take any crap from him. She might even teach him a thing or two on how to treat ladies."

"You didn't seem too happy on your date with her."

He chuckled. "Beth is okay. She's a sweet kid, really. Just young. Very young." He grimaced as he twisted the key in the ignition. "Or maybe it's just that I'm getting old. She made me feel every one of my thirty-two years. All she talked about were celebrities, and I'd never even heard of half these people."

"How come you were out with her in the first place if you're so mismatched?"

"Same as you, blind date. My stepsister set us up. I never go on blind dates anymore, but she whined until I gave in." It was as much truth as he could tell her right now. He'd promised Anne, but the fact remained that he was feeling rather guilty.

"And Beth is a friend of hers?"

"Not quite—little sister of her husband's friend, I believe. Something like that. She exhausted all the friends a long time ago."

"I see," Lea said thoughtfully. "So... You're a confirmed bachelor, are you, resisting all attempts at matchmaking?"

"Not really..." A playboy, a player and a confirmed bachelor. She had a lot of neat little boxes for him, didn't she? He shrugged. "My only crime is being single and happy to stay that way. That seems to make me fair game for anyone's matchmaking hobby."

"And why is it that you want to stay single?" She canceled the question with a gesture. "Sorry, none of my business."

"It's fine." He didn't mind giving out his standard response. "I simply like my life the way it is. Of course, if you ask my stepsister or the other matchmaking experts, they'd tell you it's just that I haven't met the right woman yet."

Lea was staring out into the night when he glanced toward her. "That's not a valid reason for being single, when you think about it," she finally said. "At our age, most people seem to have settled down with someone, even if they haven't met anyone *right*."

"That's a rather cynical thing to say, isn't it?"

"It's true."

"Yeah, I suppose it is. And some of those people have been divorced once or twice too. You know what they say about marrying in haste."

"Repent at leisure," she murmured. "Or in today's world: Divorce in equal haste, isn't it?"

There was a pause in the conversation as they parked outside a restaurant and were seated, but once they were there, Lea picked up where they'd left off, propping her chin on her hands and targeting him with a laser-sharp look. Her eyes were very green, he noticed again. Turning darker when she was excited about something. He liked them that shadowy shade of emerald.

"So," she said. "Are you saying that you think one should hold out for the perfect partner, rather than settling for someone—less perfect?"

"I don't know if I would put it like that…" Thomas grinned at her. "That would make me a soppy romantic, wouldn't it? Not exactly macho."

She smiled back. "On the contrary. I'm pretty sure romantic men are every woman's fantasy." Despite the words, there wasn't anything flirty in her voice, which was slightly confusing. Then her smile vanished and she lowered her head to stare down at the menu. "Well, it's mine, anyway. But it's tricky, isn't it? Knowing what's right. I bet a lot of those divorced people thought they'd be together forever."

"Well. People change. Life happens."

"Then there are people like my friend Anne and her husband. I don't think even continental rift could tear those two apart, ever."

"Some people are lucky."

"And some aren't." She took a deep breath and let it out in an even bigger sigh. "That's just life too, isn't it? Luck of the draw."

Thomas shifted in his chair and tried to read her face. What was behind that depressed expression and those strange questions? "I get the feeling there's a story behind that sigh. Is that the long one you were going to tell me?"

She nodded. "The short version: I thought someone was it. But it turned out he wasn't."

"I'm sorry."

She shrugged. "We broke up a while ago. I took a year out to get over him, and now he's in the past. So, now I'm trying to figure out how to date for the first time in my life." She grimaced. "Based on tonight, it's not fun."

He chuckled. "It can be fun. A lot of fun. It can also be dreadful—very dreadful. The good thing is that the dreadful bits make for excellent stories later on."

For some reason, this news seem to be music to Lea's ears. She perked up and gestured randomly, her cheeks flushed as her voice rose in excitement. "See? This is exactly why I need you!"

"Huh?" It seemed he was being unusually dense tonight. Maybe it was malnourishment. She'd drunk too much and he hadn't eaten enough. All in all, not a good basis for lucid communication. They needed food. Now. "You need me to tell you my dating horror stories?"

"Not quite—" She stopped talking when the waiter approached their table, and took their order.

Once the waiter had walked away, Lea took a deep breath and glanced around. They'd gotten a semiprivate table, and didn't have to worry much about other peo-

ple overhearing their conversation, but she still leaned
toward him and lowered her voice. "This is going to
sound pretty strange, I guess I better tell you that up
front."

Thomas grinned, feeling more and more intrigued by
the minute. What was she up to? "Don't worry. I'm
used to strange females."

"Good."

She put her hands on the table, palms up and stared
down at them as if trying to read her story from there.
"I'll be honest." She looked up. "Essentially, what all
this is about, is that I'd like to hire you for a job,
Thomas."

"A job?" he asked cautiously. "What do you mean,
a job?"

"A confidential job. Very confidential. That's an ad-
ditional reason why you're perfect for it. We're complete strangers. We don't know any of the same people,
which makes everything a whole lot easier."

Guilt tapped him on the shoulder again. So did apprehension. He should tell her about Anne now, before
this went any further.

"You see, my friends don't really understand. They
want to set me up, send me on blind dates, introduce
me to friends of their friends' friends—that was how I
ended up with James in the first place. I know they
mean well, but I'm getting so tired of their interference,
well-meaning though it is."

Damn it. He couldn't tell her, not without Anne's
permission. Anne had said Lea would be furious to find
out she'd been chaperoned. He could damage the
friendship between the two women—and he had a feeling that would mean his head on a stake in Anne's
front yard.

Yep, he had a problem.

Oblivious to his inner tug of war, Lea continued. "They'd probably think I was nuts for suggesting this—but I don't see another way."

Whoa. Earth to Thomas. Just what was he about to be drafted into here? She had paused and was looking at him as if waiting for something. He nodded. "I'm listening."

Lea took a deep breath and held it for the longest time. "Do you promise not to breathe a word of this to anyone?"

Thomas nodded. "I promise."

Her gaze searched his face, anxious, worried. It made him even more curious.

"Maybe this wasn't a good idea," she said after a while. There was hopelessness in her voice that all of a sudden made it imperative for him to let her know she could trust him. Why, he didn't know. She was a stranger.

A stranger who all of a sudden was pillaging her purse, for a tissue to hide her tears in. She was *crying?*

Cripes. What was a gentleman to do?

"Lea..." For just a second, he put his hand on hers as she nervously fiddled with the candle at the center of the table while blotting tears from her eyes with her other hand. "I know you don't know me, but if it's worth anything to you, I'm good at keeping secrets. Are you in some sort of trouble?"

"I'm sorry," she said after a while, having gained control of herself. She stuffed the tissue pack back into her purse and her smile was wavering, but brave. Her eyes were very dark now. "This is absurd. I'm a bit emotional these days. It's probably hormonal."

Emotional. Hormonal.

"I see," he said, leaning back in sudden shock. Of course. She was pregnant. Why hadn't Anne mentioned that little detail? Perhaps she didn't know. Maybe that was the big secret. He glance around the room, trying to temper his disappointment with philosophy. He'd just met the woman, for heaven's sake. Plenty more fish in the sea. But she'd been on a first date, so obviously she wasn't with the father of her child. Maybe this job Lea wanted him to do had something to do with getting the father of her baby back.

Lea's laugh was low and embarrassed. "This isn't like me. I probably shouldn't have gulped down all that wine with the appetizer. I'm afraid I've almost crossed the line between tipsy and drunk."

Wine? No, she shouldn't have. Thomas took her wine glass and moved it to the side. "You're right. You shouldn't be drinking at all. What would you like? Mineral water? Soda?"

She was looking at him strangely. "I'm not *that* drunk," she protested. "I just meant that I might be a bit more than just tipsy, or I wouldn't have been quite so...forward." She reached for her glass, but he was faster and moved it out of her reach.

"No more. Alcohol isn't good for your baby," he said firmly.

"My baby?"

"Even in small doses, it can be risky. No need to tempt fate. It's only for nine months, not a great sacrifice when everything's taken into account."

Green eyes turned darker. Dangerously darker. "What are you talking about, Thomas?"

"Your baby..." He hesitated, and wondered if he should be sliding under the table in utter·embarrassment. One of her eyebrows rose, and his suspicions were confirmed. "Oh."

"Oh, indeed."

"You're not pregnant at all, are you?"

Lea glanced down at herself and put her hand against her stomach. "I knew I'd gained weight. I haven't had time to go to the gym lately. But I didn't realize it was that bad."

"No! You're not...I'm sorry. When you said you were hormonal..." Thomas groaned. "I'm sorry. But you said you were emotional and it was probably hormonal, so I assumed you had to be pregnant."

"I'm not. I'm just hormonal. Women are. All the time. Always. As a *player*, you should know that."

"Okay." He pushed the wine glass her way. "Sorry. If we hadn't already attracted our share of attention for today, I'd go down on my knees and grovel. But have a drink." He pushed his own glass over to her side of the table. "In fact, have mine too. I'll just go straight to the strong stuff."

She grinned at last, her eyes brightening. He had the feeling his own mortification was what had cheered her up. "Don't worry, Thomas. I suppose it was a natural assumption from what I said." She shook her head. "But this isn't like me at all. Not crying in public, and not attacking strange men with weird propositions."

Finally they were back to the weird proposition. About time—and a chance to get the conversation away from his blunder. "You were going to ask me something," he said. "We've come this far—why don't you go ahead?"

"You've got a point," she said with a sigh. "I've already made a fool of myself." She sent him another slow grin. "And so have you. I suppose we might as well go all the way."

Thomas waited for her to continue. Her gaze searched his face for the longest time, as if trying to determine how trustworthy he was.

"I don't know you, do I?" she said at last, in a low voice. "The idea of putting my entire future in your hands is a bit…risky. I don't think this was a good idea."

"Your *entire future?*" What on earth could she have in mind? Thomas leaned toward her again, intrigued—and a bit nervous. "I'm becoming really curious here. What are you talking about?"

"Promise not to laugh?"

The request was childish enough to pull a smile out of him. "Yeah, I promise."

"I want a baby," she stated, and he nearly fell off his chair in shock. She didn't elaborate, just looked at him steadily.

Maybe he hadn't heard right. "You want *what?*"

She didn't answer, just stared at him with the look that reminded him of the big bad wolf.

He'd heard right the first time, hadn't he?

"You want a baby," he said, fighting back an impulse to check if the path to the exit was clear. This couldn't be what he thought it was. She couldn't be approaching a stranger, asking him to father her child. Women didn't do that, even after too many drinks. It was impossible. So impossible that there was no need for him to panic. "Okay." He nodded at her. "You want a baby. I'm with you so far."

And he wasn't laughing. This wasn't a laughing matter at all. If he did anything at all, it would be hyperventilating.

"I want a baby so bad," she blurted out. "It's crazy. I don't know where this came from, it must be biological, but it's about all I can think about. And you see, I've finally grown up. I no longer believe in romance, in Mr. Right. If he exists at all, he obviously gave up waiting and settled down with Ms. Wrong a long time ago. He's not showing. I need to be practical about this. If I want children, a family, I can't afford to wait much longer."

"I see."

"I'm thirty. Almost thirty," she amended. "Last year I ended a relationship, the only real relationship I've ever been in. Since then, my entire track record consists of the date you just witnessed."

Thomas nodded. "What have I got to do with this?" He'd just say no. She couldn't force him to…donate sperm, or whatever it was she had in mind. No problem. He'd just hear her question and say a polite no thank you. No big deal.

He leaned back and crossed his arms, waiting for the ax to fall. The things he got himself involved in.

His fear was obviously written all over him, as Lea's worried face turned surprised for a moment, and then she started laughing. "Oh, no," she said, shaking her head so hard that her dark hair swirled around her face. "Absolutely not. That's not it."

"What?" he asked, unwilling to allow her to read his mind. "What's not it?"

She was still laughing. "Relax, Thomas, it's okay. I promise that I'm not about to ask you to father my baby."

"You're not?"

Her eyes sparkled, but she bit her lip and her laughter came to a hiccupy end. "No. I'm sorry. I didn't mean to scare you. Or make you think I was completely crazy—again. Oh, God…no. I'd never ask a stranger. And certainly not someone like you.''

''Someone like me?''

''You're a multidater, remember? Practice makes perfect and all that? You're a *player*. Right? You're not looking to settle down any time soon, if ever?''

''Oh. That. Yes. Right.''

She nodded. ''Exactly. And I don't want anything to do with men like that. So you're quite safe from me. What I want is a family, so I want to find someone stable, responsible, someone who wants the same thing. You're entirely unsuitable.'' She grinned at him in a way that despite his apprehension spiked his nervous interest even more.

''Let me get this straight: you want to find someone to have children with?''

She nodded. ''Yeah. But not just that. I want what everybody has—a family. Not much to ask, is it? Everybody's doing it without much effort. I'm talking about getting involved in a serious, stable relationship that eventually might involve having a family. Not just finding someone to impregnate me.''

She said the last sentence as if it were something totally unthinkable, but he wasn't convinced. It certainly didn't sound like she was looking for a love match.

''Okay.'' He leaned back, not feeling much more comfortable knowing he was ''unsuitable.'' ''And if I'm neither genetic material nor husband material, how is it that I come into this?''

''Isn't it obvious?'' she asked, impatient. ''You know everything about this. I have to go through the dating process to find someone. You can help me cut down on the dreadful part."

"I'm not following. How would I help you through it all?"

She leaned toward him again, her eyes sincere. "It's simple. I've never really dated in my life. I want you to teach me how to. What the rules are, how to behave, what to do when, how to read men, what they want and what they mean…it's all a mystery to me. Additionally, I don't trust my own judgment anymore. Men aren't the same on a first date and two years into a marriage. Maybe there are hints. Clues. You know."

"I see," he managed to get out.

"You're probably thinking about what's in it for you. I'd hire you, as a consultant. We hire consultants all the time at work. I'll pay you what they're being paid. Which is a small fortune, by the way. And I suppose you could look at this as a learning experience too. You'd get to see things from the woman's point of view."

"I don't want your money."

"If you agree to do this, I *will* pay you. I'm not asking for a favor, I'm asking to hire you. I need your expertise. This is serious business to me, not a game."

He shook his head, feeling disoriented. "Why me?"

She was leaning toward him, excitement in her voice and her face. "You know what you're doing, don't you? You know the dating scene, what's done and what's not done. You have insight into the male mind that I lack." She fell silent for a moment before adding: "Will you do it?"

He was pretty close to speechless. "I…don't know."

She shrugged, but there was disappointment in her

eyes that he didn't like seeing. "You don't have to make up your mind right this minute, of course. You can think about it for a while if you want."

"I still don't understand why you're asking me. Why you think I'm the perfect man for this job. I'm sure you know some single men who could give you hints. Any men, for that matter, they all were single once. Husbands of your friends, perhaps?"

Her gaze traveled over him, and he felt himself still wriggling on her hook. "Well, you *are* perfect for this, aren't you? It's kind of written all over you. And the way you had the nerve to pull that stunt on our blind dates—a perfect example of supreme confidence. I was impressed." She suddenly laughed. "It was touch and go for a while if I would scream the house down, but I *was* impressed. And you look like the perfect example of the serial dater—handsome, smooth, suave…"

"Thank you," he tried to interrupt her, very much aware that the tone of her voice was not conveying any positivism toward these supposedly positive traits, and not really up to hearing more.

She continued. "Commitment-phobic, right? Not even looking for the right woman? Right?"

He nodded reluctantly. She had him pegged pretty well.

"See, you're a *player,* even if you don't know that word. Perfect for me. I bet you're a businessman, aren't you? Wheeler and dealer, right? The Dow index gets your blood pressure rising, doesn't it?"

"The Dow index…?"

"I'm sorry." Lea lowered her voice. "I don't know you at all. I shouldn't judge you. My ex was all these things. And, I admit again, I may have drunk one too many glasses of wine during the footsie session."

"If you were with your ex for years, he can hardly have been much of a commitment-phobic or a serial dater."

She narrowed her eyes and stared into her glass. "That's what you think. All that time, and he was never ready to move in together. Oh, he moved into my apartment, more or less, but he kept his and I wasn't allowed to move so much as a toothbrush in there." She swirled the wine reflectively, staring into the dark red liquid, then looked up at him with a faint smile. "I made a mistake. Or on second thoughts, maybe it wasn't a mistake at all. Anyway—I started pushing. I started mentioning settling down to one place, that there was no point in wasting rent on two apartments when we only used one."

This sounded familiar. "Did you mention having children? That sends a lot of men fleeing in the other direction if they aren't ready." It had once sent him halfway across the world. It wasn't something he was proud of, but he remembered the feeling of panic and dread at the thought of getting trapped in a relationship. He could sympathize with her ex in that area.

She shook her head. "I *thought* about mentioning having a family, but I never did. But he may have read my mind. He had an affair, that he knew I would find out about, and was extremely relieved when I told him to get the hell out of my life." She drew patterns on the outside of the wineglass with a fingernail. "I'm guessing he'd been wanting to dump me for a while but never had the guts. So he did something that was guaranteed to make me dump him."

"What a jerk," Thomas said, disgusted. Even he would never have stooped to a lousy trick like that. "That's pretty low. I'm sorry."

There was a flash of cynicism in her eyes. "You wouldn't do the same in his situation?"

"No. If I wanted out of a relationship, I'd make a clean break before jumping beds."

She shrugged, and he had the feeling she didn't believe him. "Anyway, I'm not telling you all this to get pity, Thomas. I'm over him. I guess the only thing I'm not over is my own stupidity, to have clung to him for so long."

"Well, there's a reason love is associated with the heart and not the brain."

"I don't think we'd been in love for a long time," she mused. "If ever. We were just used to each other. In hindsight, we probably stayed together so long because it was the simplest thing, not because we were particularly happy together." She shrugged. "Anyway, he was a stockbroker. For years, my emotional well-being hinged on the Dow index. I could check the Net before going home from work, and know what kind of an evening was ahead. But you're not him—I'm sorry I made that crack."

"It's okay."

"So, what's your answer? Will you be my consultant?"

Thomas leaned forward to see her face better, wondering why he hadn't already said no. "First tell me, in practical terms—what exactly is it that you want me to do?"

"There are a few things. First, help me find suitable men. I'd like to avoid more blind dates like tonight, and I'm not really sure how to go about it, how to screen them to avoid the worst riff-raff. I'd also like you to help me get through the first few dates, sort of give me hints on what to do, what not to do." She shrugged. "Be there for me to ask stupid questions that my girlfriends can't answer. Just help me get confident. Get my dating legs."

"Dating legs?" He had sudden visions he had no business seeing. "What are dating legs?"

"You know, like sea legs."

"Oh." Dizziness again. The effect the woman was having on his balance system was remarkable, and unlike her, he didn't have the excuse of too much alcohol.

"Like, tonight. I didn't even know what to do when James started acting like an eight-footed octopus. I was busy enough worrying about having to kiss him at the end of the evening."

"Maybe you worry too much about how things are supposed to be. Just let it come naturally."

"That's the point!" she said. "I don't know what comes naturally. It doesn't come naturally to me. I know that may be hard for you to understand, since this is all probably just second nature to you, but it's a complete mystery to me."

He nodded. "I see."

"Will you help me?" she asked. "Just say yes or no, I'm not pushing. No explanation needed if you don't feel like it."

She expected him to say no. It was obvious from the way her shoulders had slumped when she'd asked the question.

And of course he would say no. What else could he do? If nothing else, she would skin both him and Anne if she found out he'd been sent to chaperone her—and then kept his identity from her while she told him some of her deepest secrets and innermost feelings, thinking she was safe confiding in a stranger what she could not confide in friends.

He would say no—and with luck they'd never see each other again and the problem would be solved.

"Yes," he heard himself say instead. "I'll help you."

What had she done?

After showering and putting on one of the oversized T-shirts she liked to wear to bed, Lea grabbed the sleeping cat from the sofa and carried her to the bedroom. She needed the companionship. The satisfied sound of the cat purring always made her feel better. It calmed her down. Most of the time, it also helped her think more clearly. There was probably a medical explanation for this. If not, there should be.

Uruk hardly woke up during the transfer, just opened her mouth and yawned once, before curling up again at the foot of the bed in an identical position from the one she'd just been removed from. Lea checked the Caller ID on the phone sitting on the bedside table, and saw that Anne had called several times. It was too late to call her back now. She'd drop by tomorrow and tell her matchmaking friend all about the updated definition of "dreadful."

Feeling too jittery to go straight to bed, Lea walked barefoot to the window and rested her forehead against the cool pane. Tonight really had happened, and she wasn't sure how she felt about it, now that the exhilarating effects of having been rescued from a horror date had worn off.

She'd asked a stranger—a very attractive stranger—to teach her to date.

The effects of the wine were also wearing off—and already she wasn't sure she'd be very pleased with herself in the morning. Apart from everything else, she must have come across like a pruny old spinster, desperate to find a man. She whimpered and knocked her head softly against the window a few times. Why had he agreed, anyway? Out of amusement? He must have better things to do with his time.

He seemed nice. Very nice, she admitted. She'd felt an instant attraction to him, attraction of the kind she had been determined to ignore since he was way outside the parameters she'd set up for what she wanted.

But he'd agreed to help her. And she needed help. That much she'd learned from half an hour with James the Footsie.

She pulled the cat from the foot of the bed and settled her on the second pillow. Uruk was about the only single female she knew—so she'd have to suffer through the single-girl-talk that Lea's girlfriends no longer seemed to comprehend.

"You know, Uruk, if my plan succeeds, you'll be exiled from the bedroom again," she told the cat. "As it is, I'm just adding to my growing spinster image by talking to my cat, but since nobody is here to hear it, it's fine."

Uruk blinked a few times, then her eyes stayed wide open as she glared at her mistress. "I know," Lea said, bribing the cat with a tummy rub. "You don't like being moved around in the middle of the night when you're fast asleep. I'm sorry. But I needed to talk."

The apology was sufficient. Uruk's eyes closed and purring commenced again. She squirmed around to better accommodate the tummy rub and stretched out a paw to gently draw a claw over Lea's wrist.

"Did I do the right thing, do you think?" Lea whispered. "It's pretty unlike me to approach a stranger like that. He probably thinks I'm nuts. I mean, *I* think I'm nuts to have done that.''

What had induced her to be so impulsive? Excitement of the moment, probably. Compared to the stunt Thomas had pulled in the restaurant, it hadn't seemed so far out to enlist his help. Not until she'd seen the astonished—and alarmed—look on his face when she'd told him what she needed.

She could feel Uruk's body vibrate with the purring. The fluffy white fur on her belly was softer than anything in the world. Except perhaps a baby's downy hair.

''Sometimes, Uruk,'' she whispered, ''a woman has to do what a woman has to do. We have a mission, and we're going to get there. And anyway, it doesn't matter what Thomas thinks of me, does it? Not at all. He doesn't matter at all, does he? He's just the means to an end.''

The cat purred on and refused to take sides. Lea sighed and rolled on her back, staring up at the ceiling.

If only his eyes weren't quite so blue.

CHAPTER THREE

"DON'T ask," were the first words out of Lea's mouth when Anne yanked the front door open the following afternoon. She'd promised her friend to drop by after work and give a report on how last night's date had been. She'd be needing an apology instead. Where had they found that guy? Thanks to them, she'd had to do all of today's calculations at the office through the depressing mist of a hangover.

Then she noticed that Anne's brow was thunderous, an aura of disapproval radiating from her. She was even tapping her foot. "Hey, what's wrong? You're scowling at me."

"What's wrong? How can you ask what's wrong?" Anne retorted in what almost qualified as a yell. "I called and called last night, until eleven! I stayed up far past my bedtime to hear the news of your date."

Lea laughed. "Sorry, Mom, I didn't know I had a curfew."

Anne kept glaring at her as she held the door open. "Come in. I've been waiting to give you a piece of my mind. What the hell are you thinking?"

"What are you talking about?"

Anne gave her feelings expression by slamming the door behind her. "You went home with him, didn't you?"

"James? No way!"

"I'm not talking about James."

"Oh. You heard."

"You bet I did."

"Well, I didn't go home with the other guy either. I'm not in the habit of picking up strangers, Anne. That's probably part of my problem," she added in a mutter.

"Don't try to fool me, Lea. I'm not talking about a stranger. I'm talking about Harry."

"Harry?"

Anne picked up her son, who'd crawled toward them, and positioned him on her hip. "You're getting back together with Harry, aren't you? Did you go home with him? You did, didn't you? That's why you were still not home at ten minutes past eleven." She shook her head in disgust. "You *slept* with him, didn't you? Have you lost your mind?"

"Harry?" It no longer hurt, saying his name, Lea noticed with a kind of grim satisfaction. She really had gotten over him. "What on earth are you talking about, Anne?"

"Don't play innocent, Lea. Brian called me from work this morning. He found out about Harry through James."

Lea shook her head. Somebody, somewhere, had gotten their wires seriously crossed. She held out her arms, and Danny decided to take the plunge and dived into her arms. The child did his usual trick of kick-starting her biological clock—not that it was anywhere close to stalling. "What is this about Harry? Anne, seriously, I have no idea what you're talking about."

"Harry interrupted your date last night, didn't he? Swept you off your feet. Took you home."

"Ah." Lea started laughing, and was rather proud of herself when she realized she could laugh at the idea of Harry sweeping her off her feet. Not bad. "Oh, no,

Anne. That wasn't it at all. I haven't seen Harry in almost a year. Don't worry, he's never setting a foot into my life again. Ever.''

"Damn it," Anne muttered, the wind going out of her after several seconds of staring at her to decipher if she was telling the truth. "I mean—it's good that you're not taking that slime back—but damn it, about my sources failing." She led the way to the kitchen, mumbling to herself. "I mean, what can you trust, if not office gossip? Why would they make up a story like that?"

Why indeed. Lea felt like snickering, but she couldn't quite make up her mind whether to tell Anne about Thomas or not. "Well, I don't owe you any thanks for setting me up with that guy, James, you know."

"I take it you didn't like him?"

"He tried to put his foot under my skirt before we even got to the main course."

"His *foot?*"

"Yeah. He made it up to my knee." Danny started squirming, and Lea let him slide to the floor before sitting down at the kitchen table herself.

"Yikes. Sorry. Was that it, or did you have some major hassle with him?"

"No, I was rescued before it came to that." She just couldn't keep her mouth shut, could she? Lea castigated herself. Nope, she couldn't. She needed to tell someone about last night—and since Anne had already found out some of it, it didn't matter much. "That's where the Harry gossip comes from. James must have told Brian I was whisked away by my ex."

"Rescued? Whisked away?"

Lea fought a smile at the memory. It had been a

spine-tingling experience. "There was this guy at the next table, also on a terrible blind date, and we pretended to be lovers who'd just split up..."

Anne's mouth was hanging open. "Oh, my God. You mean the two of you ditched your dates and ran off together?"

Guilt struck again. She really needed to find out if Beth was doing okay. "Yeah."

"Wow." Anne was looking impressed. That didn't happen very often. "I have a new respect for you Lea. I didn't think you had it in you." She frowned as she poured the tea. "Why doesn't anything that exciting ever happen in my life? It's not fair, I tell you."

Lea looked down at Danny, who was trying to gnaw the foot of the table. He grinned up at her, and she noticed two new teeth. "Oh, I think you're getting plenty of excitement."

"Tell me about that guy. He sounds interesting. You got his number, didn't you? You'd better. He rescued you. You know better than to let a hero like that walk out of your life."

"I'm meeting him again tomorrow evening," she said blithely, and heard her friend squeal.

"Wow! This is terrific! Spill! I want all the gory details."

"Oh, there was remarkably little gore."

"How far did you take the pretending-to-be-lovers act?"

"Not very far."

"Did he kiss you?"

"No!" Thomas had driven her home, and said goodbye with a smile that made her insides quiver, but that had been it. Of course. After all, the poor guy had almost fainted with fear, thinking she might want him to be the father of her baby. He would probably wear a chastity belt on their next meeting, just in case.

"After all that, no kiss? Damn. Don't worry, maybe next time. Maybe tomorrow, huh?"

Lea made do with a mysterious smile, rather enjoying all this positive attention.

"Well, tell me," her friend continued impatiently. "What happened after you ditched your dates? You weren't home at eleven, so you must have been up to something."

"We had dinner together and talked."

"Until eleven?"

Lea nodded. Time had somehow vanished. After Thomas had agreed to help her out, the conversation had drifted to other things. They'd had dinner, then coffee, and she'd enjoyed herself tremendously. This is how dates are supposed to be, she'd thought vaguely at the time, and Thomas seemed to be having a great time too. Or—at least she'd assumed he'd been having fun too, but perhaps he'd just decided to start the lessons already, and all the chatting and the fun they'd had was a part of showing her the ropes?

Of course, that was it. Well, it had worked. She now had two examples of dates—terrible and terrific. All in one evening.

"Well? Tell me more, Lea! You're seeing each other again tomorrow?"

Enough was enough. She'd let her friend get the wrong idea on purpose, but she needed someone to confide in. Anne was the closest of her friends—if anyone was to know about her plan, it'd be her. "Actually, Anne, it's not what you think. I'm not dating *him*. I just asked him to help me with this dating thing."

Suspicion clouded Anne's face. "What do you mean?"

"Well…he's a player."

Anne looked blank. "What kind of a player? You mean like a football player? He's an athlete?"

Lea rolled her eyes. Didn't anybody know today's lingo? "*A player* player. He dates a new woman every night. He knows the rules and scripts. He can help me get started without making a fool of myself. Teach me how to date."

"This guy's going to teach you how to date?"

"Umm…yeah." Lea didn't like the way it sounded, coming from Anne. It wasn't *that* absurd, was it? In the course of the day, she'd almost managed to convince herself it was a logical, reasonable thing to do.

Anne was giving her a look very similar to the one Thomas had sent her last night. "He agreed to do that?"

"Yes."

Anne shook her head. "A guy wouldn't just agree to something like this out of the goodness of his heart."

"I'm paying him."

"You're *paying* him?"

"Yeah. I hired him as a consultant. This is business."

"Consultant?" Anne repeated. "I see."

"Why not? He has expertise that I need. It's logical to hire someone like that to teach me certain skills that I lack."

"Well, obviously he's interested in you. Which is great. Interesting strategy, Lea, but it might work."

Was he interested? Lea frowned. That possibility hadn't even occurred to her—not after she'd neatly filed Thomas Carlisle in the not-husband-and-father-material box. Could he have agreed to help her because he was interested in her?

No. She'd told him she wanted a baby, for heaven's sake. And he'd instantly panicked. He was a self-confessed commitment-phobic, and even if she were an irresistible siren—and she wasn't—that little piece of information on their first meeting would have most men running in the opposite direction.

"No, he's not interested, Anne, not at all. And it's not a strategy. I don't want someone like him, anyway. I'm looking for someone entirely different. Someone willing to commit."

"Men aren't willing to commit. It's not in their nature. That's why we hunt them down and tame them. See? That's what romance is all about—taming men."

"You were saying?" Brian had sidled up to Anne's back. She tilted her head back and grinned up at her husband.

"Oops. Hello, honey. Welcome home. You weren't supposed to hear that."

"Obviously not. You *tamed* me, did you?"

"Just a little bit." Anne held up her hand, a tiny gap between her thumb and forefinger, and bit her lip in a useless effort to hold back a smile. "Just a very little bit."

Lea tried not to growl as the couple kissed. Still sappily in love after all these years together. It *could* happen, obviously. Just not to her, and waiting any longer for lightning to strike was just plain stupid when time was running out.

Brian pinched a cookie and ruffled his son's hair. "You know, we just let you think you tame us. What actually happens…is something very different. Hi, Lea.

I heard all about your date last night from James. Sounds like Harry swept you off your feet.''

"No. Not Harry. Not now, not ever.''

"Not? James said so.''

"He must have said my ex. It wasn't Harry, it was someone else. I wouldn't take Harry back if he came with a lifetime subscription to Swiss chocolates.''

"I should hope not,'' Anne agreed. "Brian, I can't believe you actually believed she was back together with Harry!''

"Anne!'' Lea groaned. "You thought yourself…''

"I didn't, really. I just didn't think for a bit. Of course you wouldn't take that rat back. You're not *stupid*. She's not stupid, Brian.''

Brian held up his hands in an effort to fend off his wife's glare. "I'm just repeating what I was told.'' He yanked a kitchen stool from under the table and sat down between the two women. "I've always wanted to participate in girl talk. So, tell us, who was the guy who swept you off your feet, kissed you until your toes curled and carried you out of the restaurant?''

"Swept me…kissed me…'' Lea choked on her cookie and grabbed her teacup.

"You left out that bit!'' Anne protested. "Wow. He carried you off? Literally? And he kissed you? Right there? Wow!'' She poked her husband's stomach with her elbow. "Brian, why don't you ever do stuff like that? I'm missing out!''

"Nobody swept anyone anywhere,'' Lea coughed. "And I haven't been kissed for so long I'm not sure I remember how it's done. I can't believe this. And they say women gossip? What else did your colleagues say?''

"Let's see.'' Brian snuck a cookie down to his son,

playing on the floor. "You and the mystery man couldn't keep your hands off each other. There were some references to an inordinate amount of time you spent in his car outside the restaurant. Foggy windows and all."

Anne's eyebrows rose and Lea found herself blushing furiously without any reason at all. "That's totally untrue! We drove straight off!"

Brian shrugged. "Anyway I was supposed to thank you and that guy—what's his name?"

"Thomas."

Anne had just taken a sip of her tea, and it seemed to go down the wrong way. She sputtered, and started coughing.

"Thomas...?" Brian repeated slowly, eyebrows raised as he glanced at his wife. "Yeah? So—"

Anne's face was red, and she thumped her husband on the arm. "Stop interrogating the poor girl," she wheezed, still coughing.

"But I'm just—"

"Brian!" Anne said in a warning tone that seemed entirely overdramatic for the occasion. "Stop it. Not another word."

Brian stared at his wife for a few moments, then shrugged in a who-understands-women gesture. Anne had stopped beating her husband and was staring at Lea, but her thoughts seemed to be a million miles away. Lea waved a hand in front of her face. "Hey? Anybody home?"

Anne's gaze sharpened. "Oh. Yes. I'm here. I'm just...thinking."

"About my love life, no doubt," Lea said dryly.

Anne tilted her head and stared at her, a tiny smile starting to pull at the corners of her mouth. "Yes.

Fascinating news.'' She hesitated, and then her teasing smile grew to full proportions. ''Are you sure you weren't doing anything fun in the car with…this Thomas? Not even one little kiss? Come on. You can tell me.''

Lea had a sudden urge for another chocolate cookie and gave in to it. ''I'm positive. And I would have noticed,'' she added. Oh, yes. She would have. That smile. Those eyes. ''He's not the kind of man you'd forget kissing.''

''Aha!'' Anne was bouncing in her seat again. ''I knew it! Sparks all over the place, right?''

Lea held up a hand to warn her friend off this path. ''One or two, I admit. But I'm still not interested. I don't want a man like him. And he's not interested in someone like me. I made it clear what I'm looking for, and he doesn't fall into that category at all.''

Anne picked her son up off the floor and pushed him into his father's arms. ''Go bond, you two,'' she ordered. ''Upstairs. He needs a bath, anyway. Girl talk zone. Off limits.''

Brian obliged, and Lea watched them trot up the stairs. Father and child, Danny's arms around Brian's neck, his head on his father's shoulder. What a lovely picture. She sighed as they vanished, and dragged her mind kicking and screaming out of the fantasy world. ''You know, there's no need to kick him out of the room while we talk, when I know you'll tell him everything anyway.''

''I don't tell him *everything*. And anyway, even if I do, he's not even interested. He always falls asleep long before I'm finished with the juiciest stories. Why aren't you going after Mr. Not-the-kind-of-man-you'd-forget-kissing? He sounds exciting.''

"Exactly. He's exciting. I'm not looking for excitement, Anne. I'm dating with a very specific purpose, and this man can help me. That's it, or I wouldn't be seeing him again."

"You're taking this way too seriously."

"This isn't a joke anymore. Dating is not something I'd do for fun. It's deadly serious."

"Why? What are you talking about? I know you think it's scary to go out there again, but why deadly serious?"

Lea pointed at the baby bottles lying on the counter. "This. I'm talking about this."

Anne stared at the blue and clear plastic. "Danny's bottles?"

"Having children."

Her friend shrugged, but Lea thought she detected a glimmer of understanding in her eyes. Or was it pity? "That? There's plenty of time for you to have children…"

"No, there isn't, is there?" She put her head on the table and groaned. "I'm turning thirty soon."

"So? I turned thirty three months ago. No big deal. It's just another number."

"You have a husband. A child. Of course turning thirty is no big deal for you. I, on the other hand, have thousands of deteriorating time bombs in my ovaries, and rapidly dwindling numbers of eligible males on the market—even if I were actively searching the market. Which I'm too chicken to do."

"Today's divorce statistics predict that many of them reappear on the market after a while. Besides, you have a well-paid job that you love—not that I can imagine why you'd want to spend your life playing with numbers. You've got plenty of friends, not to mention all the time in the world to do anything you want to." Anne shook her head. "Lea, don't you know that I frequently envy you?"

"Yeah. You may sometimes wish you had my freedom. But how often do you seriously wish our positions were reversed?"

Anne reached for one of her son's toys and examined it absently. "Well, after I had Danny, that's hardly a fair question. I'm biologically bound to him and have no say in the matter. You're welcome to borrow him, though. In fact, I'd love for you to borrow him. I haven't had a romantic moment with Brian since... well, forever."

Anne didn't quite understand, did she? How could she? She'd found her soul mate before she'd even started searching, and never looked back.

"You know I'll baby-sit whenever you want."

"Thanks. I didn't know you felt that way about the big three-oh. I'm sorry." She reached for the teapot and poured herself a new cup. "I wish there was something I could do to help."

Lea shook her head wearily. "Don't feel sorry for me, Anne, I hate that. I really don't want the role of the pitiful spinster."

Anne covered her mouth to keep from spurting out the tea again. "Oh, God, Lea. Yeah, you're a real poster child for pitiful spinster, aren't you?"

"I know it's not PC to talk like this, but let's face it: I *want* a man in my life. I don't like being single. A career is not enough. I want a family. I want to get married and have children, and it isn't happening."

"It will happen. The baby's bathwater will never boil if you keep watching it."

"Excuse me?"

"I'm trying to bring originality and freshness into my speech by mixing metaphors."

"Boiling the baby's bathwater?"

"Doesn't work, huh?"

"No. In fact, you gave me a nice image to fuel my nightmares."

"Sorry. But you haven't exactly been looking, have you? There was Harry, then nothing."

"I'm looking now."

"Hmm. Well, make sure you don't focus too much on the trees and miss the Thomas."

"Miss the *what?*"

Anne looked at her innocently. "The forest. Make sure you don't miss the forest."

"Good evening, brother dear. Do you always work this late?"

Anne was sounding smug. Where had she gotten his work number, anyway? Thomas and she got along fine, but they didn't know each other all that well. His father had married her mother, when their children were already adults, and when Anne wasn't trying to set him up with a friend, they didn't associate much. He couldn't recall her ever calling him at work before.

But the mess she'd pushed him into probably warranted it. He glanced up to double-check that his office door was closed. He didn't need any witnesses to this conversation.

"Evening, Anne."

"She's cute, don't you think?"

Her voice was teasing. He could easily picture the sly grin on her face and the meaning couldn't be any clearer. Thomas pushed the keyboard out of the way and leaned on his elbows. He pushed his fingers against his temple and felt like growling at the phone.

Had this all been an elaborate setup? Was Anne hoping he and Lea would hit it off? No, that couldn't be it. Interrupting the date—meeting Lea—had been an accident, and it was entirely his own fault. He was only supposed to be there in case there was a problem. With a date of his own, for heaven's sake. But his stepsister was obviously quite pleased with the direction the evening had taken. "Nice try, Anne, but neither of us is interested, okay?"

"I owe you one, Tom. You did great. I'm impressed."

He grinned, recalling the startled look on Lea's face when he'd stormed to her table and proclaimed his love. There had been a brief moment of panic, long seconds of indecision, and then a flash of relief and humor as she'd made up her mind. And then she'd thrown herself at him, her arms weaving around his neck and her face pressed into his shoulder, and her scent had invaded his system, light and flowery, feminine and enticing. It had haunted his dreams last night, and in itself convinced him that coming to her rescue had been the right thing to do.

He cleared his throat, remembering that he had his devious stepsister on the line. "Well, there was a certain urgency to the situation. It demanded immediate action. What were you thinking, setting such a sheltered innocent up with that…slime?"

"Sheltered innocent? Wait a minute, are we talking about the same woman from the same century?"

Thomas grabbed a pen and drew random triangles on a pad. "You know what I mean. She was way out of her league. She's not used to dating, she doesn't know how to handle a creep like that guy. And you just toss her in the deep end and leave her there, expecting her to invent the lifeboat?''

''No, I didn't, Tom. Remember? I was worried about her, so I bribed and bullied my favorite stepbrother until he agreed to watch over her like a guardian angel.''

''Well, I did my part and you better do yours—find her a decent guy to make up for this disaster.''

Anne laughed. ''Yeah. Consider it done.''

Thomas stabbed the paper with his pen. She was talking about him, of course. He wasn't sure what to say, if he could object to being ''a decent guy'' for Lea. What had Lea told her? ''I'm not impressed with your taste in men, if that slime was the best you could do for your friend. He had his foot halfway under her skirt before they'd even finished ordering their food.''

''What are you yelling at me for? You're no better yourself. You left own date with that 'slime.'''

That hadn't been a nice thing to do, Thomas acknowledged with a small guilty wince. He'd have to phone Beth and apologize again, see if everything was okay. But under the circumstances, it had been the right thing to do—hadn't it? ''Big difference, Anne. Beth is a barracuda. She knows how to handle guys like that. She can put them in place by raising an eyebrow. She can take care of herself. Lea can't.''

''Sounds like you already know her pretty well. Sounds like you're being pretty protective. Not bad for someone you just met.''

The pained look on Lea's face as her feet had desperately tried to escape Footsie's clutches had gotten to him, that look of confusion and indecision as she tried subtle ways of getting her point across. He'd hardly been able to keep up his side of the conversation with Beth because he'd been too busy watching Lea and glaring at the back of Footsie's head. And when their eyes had met, and he could see she still retained a wry sense of humor about the whole thing, his reluctant fascination with her had skyrocketed.

And then it had crash-landed when she told him she was husband-and-father hunting. He drew a forceful X over the doodles on his notepad and tossed the pen into the in-tray where a dozen of its buddies were already hanging out. "I don't know Lea, but her problem was pretty obvious last night."

"It was a very knightly rescue, Tom. I'm so impressed. I think she may be too." Anne paused. "She tells me you two are seeing each other again tomorrow."

So that was still on. Lea hadn't canceled their plans after learning he'd been sent to chaperone her, and she'd told Anne about it. "Yes, she…" He fell silent. How much *did* Anne know? Had Lea told her she was hiring him for a job, or had she disguised their "lessons" as a date? Was their deal even still on, now that Lea knew the whole story from Anne? How had this become so confusing? "Anne, what did Lea say when you told her about me?"

"I didn't tell her. She told me someone named Thomas had rescued her, but I didn't tell her we knew each other. She wouldn't be happy to know I had her followed."

"What?" Thomas froze. "Anne, you have to tell her."

"Why?"

"Why? Because…it's dishonest not to. She's not going to be thrilled when she finds out." He grimaced at the phone. How much did Anne know, and how did he find out? How had he ended up in this tangle? "Anne, you have to tell her."

"Why?" she said again.

Thomas was getting a headache. How had this happened?

He flipped to a new page and jotted down the facts. Lea didn't know Anne had assigned him to be her bodyguard. Anne might not know that Lea had hired him to be her "dating consultant." He couldn't tell Anne, and betray Lea's confidence. Could he tell Lea that Anne had sent him to look out for her? No. Not without Anne's permission. Lea was too vulnerable— it had showed in her tears last night—and she'd chosen him precisely because he was a stranger.

He groaned. "Anne, why do you always have to get me in trouble?"

Anne was still sounding smug. "Lea is trouble, is she? Terrific. Can't for the life of me figure out why I never introduced the two of you before."

His computer beeped, reminding him he was supposed to be at a meeting in fifteen minutes. He reached for his briefcase and started to pile the relevant papers in. "Before? You didn't introduce us this time."

"Semantics. You got to know each other and I was the catalyst. You'll thank me someday."

He stood up, still holding the phone to his ear. "I've got to go. I have a meeting. Anne, you have to tell her we know each other, that you sent me after her."

"Why didn't you tell her yourself, anyway?"

Why indeed? "Because she's your friend, and you threatened me with blood and mayhem if I did! She's not going to take it well, coming from me, Anne. She'll feel hurt and humiliated."

"Well, I'm not doing it. There's no reason to tell her. She'll just be insulted that I thought she couldn't handle one stupid date."

"She's going to find out sooner or later. For one thing—aren't we both invited to Danny's first birthday next month?"

"No problem," Anne chirped, and he could hear Danny in the background, summoning his mother to his side. "We act all surprised at the coincidence of her already knowing my stepbrother. We never have to mention the chaperone thing. It'll be our little secret."

Thomas swore, looking at the clock. "Anne, if life has taught me anything, it's that 'little secrets' always create big messes. We'll talk later. I have to run now."

"Kiss Lea for me," Anne called as a goodbye. He slammed the phone down in response.

CHAPTER FOUR

SOMETIMES, concentrating on spreadsheets and statistical formulas was damn hard.

Why hadn't she gotten his phone number, Lea thought in frustration for the umpteenth time. Short of calling all the T. Carlisles in the phone book, she had no way of tracking him down—no way of canceling their "date." He'd driven her home, and jotted down the address, and they'd agreed he would drop by around dinnertime. It was now only four hours until then, and she'd changed her mind and changed it back three dozen times, and that was just in the two hours since noon.

She squeezed her eyes shut and whimpered. Stupid, not to have gotten his phone number. Stupid, recruiting a total stranger to help get her love life back on track. To help her find a *husband,* for God's sake!

Her grandmother's cheerful line about lemons and lemonade drifted through her head. Maybe this was for the best. She had no choice now but to see Thomas again. Maybe he'd changed his mind and wouldn't even show up. Maybe he'd just look at this as an opportunity for a funny anecdote to share with his friends—the crazy woman who wanted dating lessons so she could snare someone to father her baby.

She groaned and covered her face with her hands. He wouldn't do that, would he?

He might. She didn't know him at all, but that was an entirely possible scenario.

Work. She straightened up and pushed at the mouse to knock the screensaver away. Spreadsheets stared her in the face again, predictable and safe. You couldn't go wrong with numbers, and the only way to get through the rest of this day was to concentrate on work. Numbers and figures, estimates and probabilities.

Not blue eyes and sexy smiles.

It was raining when Thomas finally wrapped up work for the day and left the office. As always, he'd left his umbrella in the car where it gathered dust in the back seat—he wasn't an umbrella man—and by the time he'd run the minimarathon through the darkened parking lot, he was soaked. It was supposed to be summer, he thought as he reached his car, glaring up toward the heavy cloud cover. The calendar had moved to summer, anyway. When would nature catch on?

The dashboard clock told him Lea was expecting him in twenty minutes. He'd thought about calling her today and canceling the whole thing before it even started. But he'd felt compelled to keep their appointment. She'd confided in him, trusted him, even though he was a complete stranger. He'd feel like a complete heel, backing out now.

Then again, perhaps it wasn't unlikely that she'd changed her mind already. Late-night brilliant ideas, inspired by a glass of wine or two, often melted into murky puddles when exposed to the reality of the morning sun. She might be mortified at what she'd done, having confided in a stranger, asking for his help in something she considered far private to entrust to one of her friends.

He grinned as he started the car and made his way through the traffic toward Lea's neighborhood, surprised to find himself smiling in anticipation. At least this was interesting. Lea herself was interesting—if only she didn't have her heart set on finding a husband and a father for her children, something he had no plans of becoming anytime soon.

Of course, there was the small matter of Anne, and that slight deception on their part, but maybe Anne was right, and that would automatically resolve itself without any bloodshed. It certainly seemed like the easiest way out of that particular dilemma.

His doubts, almost quenched, reared their heads again and started multiplying the minute Lea opened her door, and greeted him in a quiet voice. She looked different, and it wasn't only the faded jeans and even more faded sweatshirt that had replaced the knockout skirt and blouse she'd been wearing the other night. She looked more subdued, almost withdrawn, and very vulnerable. The determination had vanished. And her smile was shy and embarrassed.

She wasn't the big bad wolf tonight. The other night, spur-of-the-moment insanity had turned them into instant buddies. But now, they were strangers.

That was disappointing.

"I think it's pretty clear that I gulped down too much wine the other night," she said with a nervous laugh once he was inside. She leaned back against the door and looked anywhere but at him. "I couldn't quite believe it when I woke up yesterday, that I'd really discussed...what we discussed." She met his eyes briefly, then looked away. "To tell you the truth, I'm embarrassed about the whole thing."

Thomas chuckled and sent her a sheepish grin in the hope of putting her at ease. He ran his hand through his hair, shaking the rain out of it. Water trickled down his neck and into his shirt, giving him goose bumps, and he grimaced. "Well, if it's any consolation, I surprised myself too. I don't make a habit out of breaking up strangers' dates."

Her tentative smile was like a slow sunrise, warm enough to chase the chill from his bones. "It was a strange evening, wasn't it? But I do appreciate you rescuing me." She looked him up and down. "Don't tell me: it's still raining?"

"A bit," he confirmed.

"Maybe you should ask someone for an umbrella for your next birthday."

"I have umbrellas," he told her. "Probably a dozen. My mother is an eternal optimist. She keeps thinking she'll end up finding one I'll actually use. So I've got big ones, tiny ones, several different colors and shapes…"

"And you hate every one of them?"

"I don't like umbrellas."

Her smile was fully grown now, filling her eyes with a warm glow. "You like being cold and wet?"

He send her a mock scowl. "Have you been talking to my mother? Those are her arguments exactly."

She cocked her head to the side and touched his jacket. The heat of her hand had to be his imagination. He couldn't possibly sense that through the wet leather. "At least your jacket should be waterproof. I'll hang it up for you."

She pushed other garments out of the way and hung the jacket so it wouldn't wet the other clothes. "Would you like tea? Coffee?" She looked at him over her shoulder as he followed her to the kitchen. "Dinner's very simple. It'll be ready in half an hour."

Thomas was distracted by a huge black cat rubbing

against his ankles. He bent down and scratched the animal's neck.

Lea glanced back when he didn't answer, and raised an eyebrow. "Or perhaps a hot water bottle and an electric blanket would be more appropriate? Actually, Uruk can function as both."

"Uruk?"

"Sharp claws, sharp teeth. She's halfway to being an uruk-hai."

"A what?"

"You know, Tolkien?"

"Ah. Right."

"Coffee?"

He nodded. "Coffee would be great." He picked up the fantasy cat, who was begging for more attention, and brought it along.

Lea's apartment was small, but warm and cozy, every inch of it he'd seen so far. She was a nester, he decided. She'd make a great mom for that kid she wanted so badly. Christmas cookies and bedtime stories and all the hugs a kid could possibly need.

There were quite a few things out of place though. He stopped at the entrance to the kitchen to examine a huge rock perched on a shelf. It had bits of kitchen utensils stuck to it.

"Lovely, isn't it?" Lea asked. "It's by a local artist."

Thomas tried to think of a polite adjective. "It's...different."

She nodded. "Yes. It spoke to me the minute I saw it. It's called *Distance*." She pointed across to another horrid sculpture on a lower shelf. "See that one? It's my favorite. Can you guess what it's called?"

Thomas stared at the object. It looked a bit like a

bird. If you squinted, and ignored the barbed wire running through the entire thing. "No. No idea."

"Really? I think it's obvious." She patted the object on its...beak. "It's called *Flash*."

"Flash," Thomas repeated. He squinted again, trying to see why that thing could be called Flash, and why that name would be obvious. Nope. Couldn't see it.

Lea was looking at him with half a grin. "You hate the sculptures, don't you?"

"No...I..." He choked on the lie and shrugged. She'd seen through him anyway. "Okay, yes. I hate your sculptures. Not my kind of thing. But then I know nothing about art."

"But you know what you like, right?" She was grinning widely now, and he realized he was probably not the first person to insult her art collection. They entered the kitchen, which was mercifully empty of artistic sculptures.

"I've been doing a lot of thinking," Lea said, her back to him as she fiddled with the coffeemaker. The glossy dark hair was in a loose ponytail now, swinging softly as she moved her head. He remembered how it had felt soft and warm against his fingers. "I was going to call you and cancel everything, but I didn't have your phone number." She turned around to face him. Behind her, the coffeemaker began to gurgle. She looked at him for a while, as if checking just how pleased he was to be off the hook. He waited for her to go on. The cat was demanding all his attention, anyway.

"But then I changed my mind," she finally continued, her voice hesitant and questioning. "Half-drunk and shell-shocked or not, I did have a point. It's not such a bad idea, logically thinking. I mean, if you're still up for it, I'd like to go ahead with that crazy plan of ours.'' Her laugh was tremulous. ''Even though it is pretty crazy, isn't it?''

He leaned back against the counter and nodded, surprised to find himself relieved that she wasn't canceling their plans. ''I haven't changed my mind. Actually, I think it could be fun for both of us. We'll look at it as a game, okay?''

''Oh. Great. That's…terrific. Wonderful.'' The look on her face and the way she was wringing her hands together suggested she was not being quite truthful about this being great, terrific and wonderful. She'd been counting on him to back out, he realized, hoping he'd be the one to do so.

''I made some notes.'' She pointed toward the kitchen table, and he could see it was strewn with pieces of paper torn from a notebook. ''Last night. I couldn't sleep, so I started making plans. I'm not sure it makes an awful lot of sense, but it's a place to start, anyway…''

Thomas gestured toward the table, when it didn't seem like she would say anything more. She had the trapped look again. ''Should I take a look?''

''Yeah…'' Her shoulders lifted in an uncertain shrug. ''I suppose. It's just ideas, possibilities, problems, all sorts of things. Not a brilliant battle plan or anything.''

He put the cat down on the floor and reached under her small kitchen table—obviously used by only one person—and pulled out a stool. He sat down and bent over the open notebook, then glanced up again. He knew so little about her. Anne hadn't said much, and last night they hadn't exactly been exchanging basic information. "What do you do at work, by the way?"

"At work? Oh…I'm a statistician," she said, sounding like the question had surprised her. They hadn't talked about this the last time. Everything else under the sun, but not work. "I work at an insurance company. You?"

"I'm rather chagrined to admit that you were right— I do fall under the general category of businessman." He grinned at her. "I'm a corporate lawyer. I don't have my heart or any other vital organs tied to the Dow index, though."

Lea felt her cheeks warm in a blush at the reminder. She'd blathered about her ex to him. She'd *cried,* for heaven's sake. In front of a strange man, in a public restaurant. What had gotten into her? She turned away and poured them both coffee. The dinner was in the oven, it would take care of itself for the next half hour.

When she looked up again, Thomas was squinting at her notebook, obviously trying to decipher her handwriting. He was in for a challenge. Fine. Maybe that would distract him from the actual contents.

"Milk? Sugar?" she asked.

He glanced up. "Huh? Oh. The coffee. No, black is fine, thank you."

Lea swallowed as she sat down opposite him. Were men supposed to have these effects, just by looking up and flashing a smile? Maybe she'd been out of circulation far too long. She couldn't remember Harry ever having quite this effect on her.

"Looks like you've been doing a lot of thinking," Thomas said, turning the page.

Lea nodded. The scribbled pages held her thoughts,

her worries and concerns, problems and attempts at solutions. Generally it was something she wouldn't show to anyone, not even her closest friends. It was too private and personal.

But she was showing it to Thomas without much reservation. This was business. Professional. He was going to help her, and he needed to know all the facts. She didn't have a very firm basis for trusting him, but she was going with her instincts. Nothing ventured, nothing gained—right? That was what this whole thing was about in the first place. Taking chances. And he was a stranger. Even if he talked about her behind her back, it wouldn't be to anyone she knew.

"Yeah," she replied. "Insomnia will do that to you. Things never look quite as bleak as they do at three o'clock in the morning, do they?" She grabbed the notebook and turned it around so she could see it. "Could you read my handwriting at all?"

Thomas chuckled. "Not really. I could make out some key words, but that was about it."

"Don't worry. Everybody has trouble with my handwriting." She stared at the scrawled notes. They looked more stupid now than they had in the middle of the night. "I can barely read it myself, which sometimes is a blessing. Anyway…the first step. I guess that would be deciding on a plan to meet guys in the first place." She looked at him. He still wasn't laughing. Not even looking at her as if she were completely nuts. Which she probably was. So far, so good. "Right?"

"Right."

"Do you have any suggestions?"

"You mean, avenues to meet people?" He shrugged in response to her nod. "I'm not sure. What do you have in mind? Are you thinking about formal or informal ways?''

She shrugged. ''I don't know.''

''Don't you know some guys you find interesting?''

''Not…really.''

He put his elbows on the table and grabbed one of her pens. He kept his head slanted down, but looked up into her eyes. The effect was strangely penetrating and she leaned back, crossing her arms. ''You told me you'd been single for about a year,'' he said. ''Men must have asked you out during that time.''

''Well, yes. A few.''

''And you turned them down.''

''Yes.''

''Why?''

She held her breath for a minute, trying to compose an answer that would make sense to him as well as herself. ''I wasn't ready. I didn't want a rebound relationship. It seemed too complicated and risky. I was…''

''Afraid.''

She was annoyed to find she was biting her lip again. She was even more annoyed that he'd hit the nail on the head in that soft, challenging voice. ''Yes. Okay, you're right. I was afraid.''

''Of what?''

''I know what you're getting at.'' She moved restlessly. ''I know what you mean.''

''Do you?''

''Yes. You're thinking I'm using my inexperience at the dating game as an excuse, and that I'm really afraid of getting emotionally involved again.'' She heard her own voice end the sentence on a question mark, and whatever else she'd planned to say vanished from her mind. Was that it? Had she been lying to herself? Had she been tangling herself up in practical problems, and not realizing where her real fears were hidden?

"I'm no Freud, but, yes, that sounds logical."

Her mug had lost its handle, years ago. She fiddled with the familiar scar in its side. "It doesn't matter, does it? This time, I'm letting logic prevail. Emotions cannot be trusted, can they?"

"No," he said softly. "I suppose they tend to lead us astray." He underlined some of her scrawled words. "Security. Stability. Endurance. That's what you're looking for in a relationship?"

"Yes."

"Okay." He pulled out another paper. "And to get there, your plan is to meet several candidates and interview them to see how compatible you are."

She grimaced. "Sounds clinical, doesn't it?"

He looked up and flashed her another lightning grin. "No. That's essentially what dating is all about, isn't it? What you're doing is just a bit more conscious, but that's it—meeting people, and seeing how you get along."

"You don't think I'm nuts?"

He laughed then. It sent a tremor down her spine. "Nah. Well, you had me worried for a minute the other night, but I'm over it. Tell me about those men who've been asking you out. Any of those you think you'd like to date now?"

"I don't know. I don't think so. Many of them have girlfriends now. And anyway, I couldn't possibly ring them up and say yes to a date they asked me out on eight months ago!"

"Why not?"

"Why not? Because—because…" Why did all the

logical reasons escape her right now? "I just can't do that sort of thing. Do you?"

Thomas shrugged. "I might. If the circumstances were right. I mean, what have you got to lose?"

"It's not fun, being rejected!"

"Well, that's life. It's full of rejections and let-downs. You just muddle through it all nevertheless."

She shook her head, her lips a tight line. "I couldn't call them. No. Too aggressive. It's not me."

"Okay. You could get involved in some social activities where you're likely to meet a lot of people. Classes, sports, whatever."

"That's too complicated. And I don't have the time."

His look told her she was being difficult. "I could tell you that if you don't have time to socialize, you don't have time for a boyfriend or a husband, let alone a family, but okay. Then that leaves us with formal venues. There are reputable dating agencies. Online dating. And personal ads, of course."

Her stomach protested at each of these three suggestions. The prerequisite for this entire mission, her own enthusiasm, was noticeably missing in action. "I don't know. They all sound dreadful. Like I'm in for series of blind dates stretching infinitely into the horizon."

"I hear there are some excellent dating agencies out there."

"Have you used them yourself?"

"No. Have you?"

"No!"

"Then you know nothing about them. Cut the prejudice. Why not give it a try? It's a quick method, and if we do it right, it's safe. And if it doesn't work out, no harm done.''

Her stomach was still doing flip-flops. This was scary. How could he be sitting there, all relaxed and serious, when she was freaking out over here? ''I don't know. I'm getting icy feet.''

Thomas put down his pen and laid his palm on top of it, rolling it back and forth, his blue gaze steady on her. ''Maybe this isn't what you really want, Lea.''

''Of course it's what I want. I told you, yesterday.''

''And you're telling me something entirely different now.'' He paused and looked down at the notebook. ''You know, if a baby is all you're after, you do have the option of doing that without a man.''

She shook her head so hard her vision blurred. ''No. No way. This isn't just about that. I want more than a baby. I want a family. I told you—I'm not just looking for someone to impregnate me, Thomas. I don't want my child to grow up without a father.''

''Relationships break up all the time. There are no guarantees that families last. Hiring a 'consultant' won't make it any more likely that you'll find Mr. Right.''

Mr. Right. Hadn't they already had a little talk about Mr. Right? ''Don't you get it? I told you—I'm not looking for Mr. Right. Just someone who wants the same things that I do.''

''Babies?'' The skepticism in his eyes sparked a frown on her face.

''Well, I want a family. Stability. There must be men who want that too. I know there aren't any guarantees, but if I do this correctly I can maximize my chances for success.''

Thomas laughed again. His laugh did funny things

to her stomach. "Right—you're a statistician. But you'll have to be careful not to bring the subject of babies up too soon."

His last words held a strong hint of warning. She couldn't help but laugh. "Don't worry, I'm not about to put their father skills to test on the first date."

"Make sure you don't."

"I can ask them if they want children eventually, can't I?"

"No! Not at all!" He leaned forward and held up a finger. "The Rule of Rules: You don't mention babies. Not on first date, not on tenth date, not for at least a year."

"A *year*? That's a bit long, isn't it?"

He shook his head. "It's the minimum. Take it from me: you'll scare them off. Men are commitment-phobic at heart."

"But that's the point—I'm looking for someone who isn't! And I need to know sooner than a year. Maybe there's a subtle way of bringing up the subject…"

"Bring up the subject of a baby before he's ready, and no matter how perfect your prince is, he's likely to bolt."

This didn't sound encouraging. "Thomas, if I meet someone through an agency or personal ad, it's natural for us to ask each other about what sort of a life we want. Having children or not is one of the biggies. I *have* to ask."

He shrugged. "At your own risk, then. Don't blame me for the consequences. I warned you. If he brings it up—fine, but if you do, expect that to be the last you'll see of him. Your choice."

This sounded serious. And, of course, he should know. She sighed. "Okay. No baby talk. At least not on the first couple of dates. After that, I'm not making any promises. These are things that need to be discussed early on, or we'll be wasting our time."

He nodded. "Which brings us back at square one: how to meet men."

Lea whimpered and slumped over until her forehead hit the table.

"I suppose I could set you up with some friends of mine…" she heard Thomas say.

"No." She straightened and shook her head. "That would be too weird, especially if I hit it off with one of them. Just strangers."

"Okay. Why don't we give a dating agency a try, then?"

She squeezed her eyes shut at the thought. "Oh, God."

"Do you want to pick one, or shall I?"

She pointed with her eyes closed. "The Yellow Pages is on the third shelf over there. My computer is in the lounge. Help yourself."

In her self-imposed darkness, she heard his chair scrape across the linoleum as he rose and the rich sound of his chuckle. Then his hand touched her shoulder in a pat. "Don't worry. This won't be so bad. Come on, let's check online."

"So, you've never tried these agencies yourself?" she asked when they'd been browsing for a while.

"No."

"You've had some nightmare dates, though, haven't you?"

"Hasn't everybody?"

"Tell me about the most horrible date you've been on."

His profile showed that his eyes were steady on the

screen, but his cheek tightened in a grin. "No. I've repressed the memory. Dredging it up will cause untold psychological damage. To both of us."

"Come on, tell me. How bad was it?"

He glanced toward her and gave her another sample of that stomach-twirling grin. His arm brushed hers as his hands hovered over the keyboard. "You're procrastinating because I'm waiting for you to tell me your vital statistics."

She looked at the screen and blinked in shock. "This isn't a proper dating agency. It's a sleazy dating site. See that picture?"

Thomas shrugged. "It was the first thing the search engine pointed to. We're just feeling our way through this. Typing in your age and interests isn't going to kill you." He stood up. "Sit in this chair. It's better if you do the typing."

Reluctantly she changed chairs with him and entered her age—29 for a few more precious weeks—and some vague interests.

"Books, gardening, cooking and baking," Thomas read with a frown.

"Something wrong with that?"

"No. But it makes you sound thirty years older than you are."

"Plenty of younger women like to bake and do gardening! That's just a prejudiced stereotype."

"Even so, it's true. What about some other interests? Movies? Music? Dancing? Romance?"

She grimaced. "I suppose."

"Which?"

"All, I guess. Except romance," she added. "I don't want to give the impression that I'm a romantic looking for true love. Just a compatible life partner."

"Not true love, just a compatible life partner," Thomas muttered. "Fine. Type away."

"Why do I get the feeling you disapprove?"

"I don't disapprove, exactly. It's sad to see someone so disillusioned and cynical."

"You're not exactly Mr. Happily-ever-after yourself, are you?"

"It could happen."

She stopped typing to stare at him. "Really?"

Thomas shifted in his chair, looking uncomfortable. "Well, it could. I guess. Eventually. Everything's possible. Maybe when I'm a bit older. No way until I'm at least thirty-five. I'm not settling down sooner than that."

"You believe in love?"

He grinned. "I think I have a similar feeling about love as I did about Santa—it may be there, and there is a lot of circumstantial evidence, but I'm withholding judgment until presented with some rock-solid proof."

"You were a cynical kid, huh?"

"No. Just a logical one."

"Hmm. Well, Mr. Spock, I've registered and given my data. What now?"

"Play around. See if there's anything interesting." He had the Yellow Pages on his lap and was flipping through it. He stopped at D. Her stomach protested yet again. "Thomas…"

He looked up and his blue eyes narrowed as he honed in on her fears. "Relax, Lea. Nothing's going to happen against your will. We're just doing some preliminary research. Play with your computer while I look at the Yellow Pages. Who knows, maybe your soul mate is just a click away."

She grunted in objection, but reluctantly obeyed,

asking the computer for a list of men that matched her information.

"Goodie," she muttered. "Here's a guy—to use the term loosely—who's had a sex change operation, but then changed his mind. He's looking for a woman who doesn't mind his missing certain bits of anatomy."

Thomas didn't even look up. "Well, since you're looking for someone to father a baby, I suppose that rules him-slash-her out."

Lea scrolled down, dismissing each in turn. "My God, I never knew there were so many weirdos in the world. And I'm turning into one of them."

"You're not a weirdo."

Lea was staring at yet another character profile. "Oh, God. I could become someone's third wife, if only I had red hair. The brunette position is already filled."

"Okay. That's enough." Thomas reached over and stole her keyboard. He closed the window with the picture of the polygamist and his two wives, and started tapping on the keys. "Maybe this wasn't a good place to start after all. But some of those reputable dating agencies have Web sites. Let's check them out."

There wasn't much information on those sites, so they resorted to the phone book again. Lea circled the number for a couple of agencies that sounded promising and looked up at Thomas with a "now what" expression on her face.

Thomas pointed at the small ad. "They answer the phone until nine in the evening. Go ahead, get it over with."

Lea whimpered, and glanced toward the phone. Thomas stood up and fetched it. "Here you go."

She held the phone in the palm of her hand. "I'll call tomorrow morning."

He tilted his head and grinned at her. "Will you?"

"Yes. Maybe. It could happen."

"No time like the present. Give me that phone. I'll do it." He snatched the phone away from her and punched in the numbers. He put the phone to his ear, still grinning, but a few seconds later he shoved it at her and moved away.

He'd pay for this little trick, Lea vowed, grinding her teeth as she tried to make sense to the person on the other end of the line.

But it just took ten seconds for the receptionist to take down her name and give her an appointment. She slammed down the phone and took a deep breath. "I did it. I actually did it, I have an appointment at a dating agency."

"Terrific," Thomas said, clasping her shoulder and squeezing. "That wasn't so hard, was it?"

"Well—yes. It was."

He chucked. "When's the appointment?"

"The twentieth, five o'clock."

"The twentieth."

"Yup."

"That's almost two weeks from now!"

Lea made a show of checking the computer calendar. "Yes, so it is."

Thomas leaned back, crossed his arms and gave her a hard stare. "You're procrastinating."

"No. I'm giving myself enough time to prepare."

"To worry. To toss and turn, wondering if you're doing the right thing."

She frowned at him. "When did you get to know me so well?"

Thomas shook his head. "This wasn't a wise decision."

"Well, it's done."

"You could call back and ask for an earlier appointment."

"Nope. This will give us plenty of time to prepare."

"Okay. They're probably going to ask a lot of questions," Thomas said. "Maybe we should talk about what you're looking for."

Lea shrugged. "I'm looking for someone nice."

"'Nice.' I don't think that's a searchable quality in their databases."

She stretched, then folded her arms. "Just a normal guy. Someone not terrible, just a nice, normal guy. That doesn't seem like a tall order, does it?"

"What about age, looks, interests, occupation?"

"Close to my age," she allowed. "I don't want someone who's much older or younger. Could get too complicated."

"Okay, what about looks?"

She shrugged. "I have no particular preferences. I'm not picky. Just a normal nice-looking guy. Doesn't have to be gorgeous, but wouldn't hurt if he was okay looking, of course."

Thomas's pen hovered over the notepad, but he wasn't writing anything down.

"Interests?"

"Preferably no all-consuming interests, but otherwise I'm pretty much open-minded."

He dropped the pencil on the table in resignation. "Okay, I give up. I hope the people at the agency have more luck narrowing down what you want."

"I'm just flexible," she objected. "That has to make it easier, right? How exactly do you suppose they find a match for someone?"

"I suppose they'd match some of your interests, and

taking account of your world views, politics and other issues, might be smart.''

"Yes. But I hope they don't match too much. Opposites attract, you know.''

"I know.''

"You're coming with me, right?''

"To the agency? Why?''

"You're a part of this.''

He shrugged. "Sure. I'll come with you.''

"Oh—while I remember, I owe you a check for this week.''

"I told you, I don't want your money.''

"I don't want you to do this as a favor to me, Thomas. I want it to be professional. Business.'' She retrieved her checkbook and quickly wrote the check. She'd already calculated the time Thomas had spent on this, and checked the going rate for the consultants her firm hired. It was a steep amount, but it was worth it. "Here you go.''

He looked at the check and blinked. "Wow. It's a wonder anyone can afford me.''

"It's just a standard consultant fee. And you better cash it,'' she warned him.

"I'll make good use of it,'' he said blandly and tucked the check into a shirt pocket, but there was a glint in his eyes that she didn't trust. She made a mental note to check with her bank.

A timer went off in the kitchen and Lea jumped to her feet. "Dinner's ready. Come on, after all this we deserve food.''

Over dinner, Lea changed the topic of conversation on him, her green eyes narrowing on his face as her fork paused.

"What about you, Thomas, what are you looking for?"

"What do you mean? Romantically?"

"Yes. Do you actually like dating?"

"Sure. It can be fun."

"What do you like about it?"

"Getting to know people, spending an evening with someone. It's fun. At least some of the time."

"What are you looking for in a woman?"

He grinned at her. "Are you thinking about returning the favor and asking the agency to find me a wife?"

"No, I suppose that wouldn't work, since you're not looking. Don't you want a family? Kids?"

"Maybe someday. I made a vow a long time ago that I wouldn't settle down until I was thirty-five at the very least."

"Why thirty-five?"

"I was nineteen at the time." He pushed a pea around his plate and frowned. "Now that I'm approaching thirty-three, maybe it's time to reconsider, but at the time I thought I'd be an old and decrepit man at thirty-five. My life would be over anyway, so I might as well spend it on raising kids."

She looked scandalized. "You don't like children?"

"Sure. I've got nephews and nieces. I love them."

"Then why did you say…"

He shrugged. "I was nineteen. My brother was getting divorced at the age of twenty-three, leaving two kids in a split family. Our parents had a similar history, and we grew up without our father. I just think people jump into this far too soon, and they end up hurting their children."

"And you haven't changed your mind all this time?"

"I haven't had an occasion to do that, no. I like my life fine the way it is."

"No special woman in all this time? There must have been."

He hesitated. "There was, once, but it didn't work out. She wanted—" Aw. This probably wasn't a story to share right now. He cleared his throat. "Anyway, we should get back to our list, shouldn't we?"

"Kids…?" she finished with a dawning horror, her eyes widening. She put her fork down and leaned back, pulling away from him in an unconscious avoidance. "She wanted kids, and you didn't? That's what you were going to say?"

Thomas nodded, feeling like the lowest scoundrel as he felt her pitch him into a box with her ex. It was a choice he had made, and although he had been controlled by his emotion more than his head, he didn't regret it. At the time, panic had set in. He hadn't been able to imagine settling down to raising a family and Sheila had been so determined. "Yeah. I wasn't ready. So, we split up and I moved to Germany for a year."

"Germany?" She dropped her fork again and it clanged against her plate. "You moved to *Germany?"*

"Er…yes." In retrospect, this seemed a bit of an overreaction.

"Germany, Europe—a country on the other side of the world?"

"That's the one."

"Are you telling me that you moved to *Germany* to get as far away as possible from a woman who wanted to have your children?"

"There was an opening for a job there, and I took it," he mumbled, stabbing a potato with his knife. "The relationship was over. It seemed like a good time to get away for a while. Reflect on my life and where it was going. And drink lots and lots of foreign beer, of course.''

Lea's eyes were still wide open, staring at him. ''You told me I couldn't bring up the subject of children for at least a year. How long was it before your girlfriend did?''

Thomas stalled, unwilling to answer the question. ''A while.''

''That means more than a year,'' Lea assumed, very accurately. She groaned. ''See what I have to deal with? One wrong step, and my prince will pack up and move to Timbuktu. Why are men so difficult?''

Men?

Thomas didn't say it out loud, but he was pretty sure Lea could read the opposite question on his face.

Why were *women* so difficult?

CHAPTER FIVE

"IT's their Y-chromosome," Anne explained, squinting to read the fine print in the flour-smudged cooking book she had open on the kitchen table. "You know, a Y-chromosome is really an X-chromosome with one arm missing. No wonder they're a bit helpless, poor things. But once you have them tamed, it must be said—they do have their advantages." She flipped a page. "I think I'll be making a cake in the shape of a snake for Danny's birthday. He has a stuffed one and adores it. What do you think—vanilla or chocolate frosting?"

Lea groaned. "Anne, we're talking about men, not dogs. I'm not denying that there may sometimes be certain similarities in their behavior—both in a good and a bad way—but I'm not going to be running an obedience school at my home, you know."

"Chocolate or vanilla?"

"Chocolate, naturally. The kid is turning one year old, you can't inflict vanilla upon him. Bake the child a chocolate snake. Why are you doing this now, anyway? His birthday is weeks away."

"Yes, but I've never baked a snake before, so I'd better make a practice one. Chocolate it is. And don't knock obedience training. You've never properly lived with a man, have you? Just wait until your floors are carpeted with dirty socks. You'll be reading up on behavior modification soon enough." She grinned evilly, not looking up from her book. "And you're already searching the kennels for a stray, aren't you?"

Lea sent her friend an accusing stare. "Anne! I thought you were going to be understanding and supportive about my plight, and here you are, making fun of my mission."

"Sorry. Supportive and understanding. Right. I forgot for a minute."

"Maybe Thomas's sperm bank idea wasn't a bad one after all," Lea muttered. That got her friend's nose out of the cookbook.

"He suggested you go to a sperm bank? Are you serious?"

"No, he didn't. Not really. He just pointed out that if all I wanted was a baby I didn't need to go through the whole dating rigmarole."

"He's right."

"That road may be fine for some women, but not for me. I don't just want a baby. I want a family. I don't want to introduce my children to test tubes when they ask about their father."

Anne was giving her the wicked look again. "But what about him? Thomas? You saw him again last night, didn't you? What's he like? Any particular second impressions?"

"He's...nice enough." Yeah. Nice. That was it. A *nice* guy who'd flee halfway across the world, and not stop until Germany when faced with the prospect of committing to a woman. Maybe this hadn't been a good idea at all. How could a guy like that help her find his exact opposite?

"Aaaaand...?" Anne prompted.

"No." Lea shook her head firmly. "Definitely not. Put that idea right out of your head. He's utterly wrong for me. Just the thought of settling down is horrifying to him. He's not even going to think about it until he's thirty-five.''

''But you do like him?''

''He's likable enough,'' she said. She'd have to be careful not to give too much away. She might be attracted to Thomas, but it was something she'd fight. It wouldn't help to give Anne any ideas.

''Elaborate, will you?''

''Did I mention that he's got a smile that'll melt the polar ice caps?'' Lea groaned and buried her blushing face in her hands when she realized what she'd said.

Weak. She was weak, betraying her own feelings by blurting out stupid things like that.

''Wow,'' Anne sighed. ''You mean he makes your knees turn to jelly and all?''

Lea nodded miserably. ''Afraid so.''

''Mmm. Good. Extremely promising. Are you sure he's not trainable?''

''Positive. You should have seen the look on his face when I told him I wanted a baby. And I wasn't even saying I wanted *his* baby. He's not a suitable stray at all. Forget it.''

''Well, a slight baby-phobia is only to be expected from any man, you know. It took Brian a while to come around. They change their minds after a while.''

Lea shook her head. ''Forget it. Thomas is…well, whatever he is, I'll make do with ogling from afar.''

''And some sizzling fantasies, I hope.''

Lea pretended not to hear her friend's teasing, although she suspected the heightened color in her cheeks was giving her away.

Those hadn't been *fantasies*…exactly. Just involuntary images flashing through her head when she least expected it. Neurons randomly firing, that was all. They weren't *fantasies*. "I'm not going for looks, charm or sex appeal. Just someone nice, responsible, stable."

Anne made a face. "Dull."

"If the only way I can get nice, responsible and stable, is through dull, I'll take that."

"You know, they do make the nice, responsible and stable model with interesting also thrown in."

"Show me one, and I'll try it out."

"Sorry, but I'm still using mine. The responsible and stable part of them is often buried beneath the surface. You have to work for it. You may have to dig deep, but it's worth it."

"I'm not sure I want to know what your courtship with Brian was like."

Anne chuckled, a new light coming into her eyes. "It was…interesting. Just ask him. In retrospect, I believe he even enjoyed the chase and the capture."

"Who was being chased?"

"He did the chasing. I did the capturing. Fair division of labor, if you ask me."

"You think you'll be together forever, don't you?"

"I know we will."

Lea stared at Anne's cookbook, now displaying a picture of an edible crocodile. Together forever. No hesitation, absolute certainty. Was it all just an illusion? "Anne… Do you ever worry that Brian might cheat on you?"

Anne didn't look shocked at the question, more like astonished. "No. I know he wouldn't. Why?"

"Tomorrow would have been the twelfth anniversary of my relationship with Harry," Lea said. "And a year and a week since we split up."

"You mean he... Oh, Lea, I never knew that was the reason you split up. Why didn't you tell me?"

"I was embarrassed," she muttered. "I know, stupid, but in the beginning I blamed myself. Just like he did."

Anne slammed the cookbook shut, fire flashing in her eyes. "He cheated on you, then blamed you for it? That rotten...if my son weren't playing under the table I'd tell you exactly what I think of that jerk. If I ever see him again..."

"Forget him, Anne. I have. I've moved on to greener pastures."

"You sure have. Not only that, but it sounds like you already have a prime example of a stallion grazing there."

"Anne!" Lea groaned, barely resisting the impulse to snatch up the cookbook and beat her friend over the head with it.

"Sorry. I couldn't resist. What's up next for you and your...mentor?"

"I have an interview at a dating agency scheduled soon. He's coming with me."

"Seriously?"

"Yes."

"Should be interesting," Anne muttered.

Lea whimpered. "Actually, I can do without interesting."

"You're not seeing Thomas before then? To go over strategy, or something?"

Lea shook her head. "Why should I? I don't need him before then."

Wrong.

"Thomas—you didn't need to come over. I told you

it was nothing. You sounded so busy. I'm feeling guilty here.''

Thomas had already gotten rid of his jacket and thrown it over the usual chair. He sat down on her sofa, glancing at his watch. ''I was passing through this part of town, so it was no problem stopping by. I need to be somewhere else in an hour though, but this sounded urgent. What's up?''

She sat down in the recliner opposite him, wondering what to say. The original reason for her to call him at work, at eight in the morning, seemed rather trivial now. ''Nothing really…'' She'd asked if they could meet for a chat after work. He'd sounded busy, and asked if he could get back to her. It was already evening, and since this morning, she'd decided it had been a stupid idea after all. It was probably a good idea to start sleeping on ideas before presenting them to Thomas. ''I feel a bit stupid, calling you up like this.''

''I thought we'd agreed you'd stop calling yourself stupid.''

''I am stupid when it comes to this. I have a subzero Dating IQ.''

Thomas frowned, telling her she could expect limited sympathy on this issue. ''Stop wallowing and tell me what's wrong.''

Lea slid even further into her recliner and hunched over, folding her arms over her middle. ''Last night— I woke up from this horrible nightmare…''

''Ouch. Sorry,'' Thomas said sympathetically.

''Want to guess what it was about?''

''Let's see…my last nightmare was about a giant spider was spinning a cocoon around me. Something like that?''

''Uh, no. Worse.''

"Worse?"

"I was on the phone, calling that date they're finding for me—and I didn't know what to say."

"I hardly think that's worse than being eaten alive by a giant spider."

"You don't understand. I was frozen, paralyzed…"

"Speaking of paralyzed, do you have any idea what spider's poison does to you?"

"Thomas!"

He grinned, his forearms on his thighs and hands clasped together as he leaned toward her. "Okay. I'm listening. Then what happened?"

"Nothing. I woke up, sweating and terrified, and realized it would be just the same for real. I don't know what to say. And I do have to make the call—according to the mini-lecture I received over the phone, I'm supposed to be the one to ask him out, to pick a place to meet—"

"Lea…this really isn't such a big deal."

"It is. Can we go on a practice date?"

"What do you mean?"

"I want to do it all, as a practice. From calling you up, to saying goodbye. Everything."

"Playacting?"

"Yes."

He leaned back, his expression not promising. "I'm really not good at acting."

"Just imagine I'm someone you're dating. You're the expert. Just sort of blank out my face when you look at me, and imagine one of your Beths."

"One of my *Beths?*"

Lea waved a hand. "Whatever."

"I was never interested in Beth," he objected.

"Never mind Beth. How about it? I know this

wasn't a part of the initial job description, but it'd make me feel much better.''

He stared at her for a while. "Sure. Okay. We'll go on a practice date."

Lea smiled and reached out to squeeze his arm. "Great. Thanks. You're such a good sport. I'm voting you employee of the month, that's for sure. Tomorrow?"

"Sure. Where do you want to go?"

Lea frowned at him. "You're the expert. Where do people go on first dates?"

Thomas shrugged. "There are a million possibilities."

Lea groaned. "See my problem? A million possibilities and all I can think of is going to a restaurant or a café, maybe a movie. What else is there?"

"Just about anything. You could go a concert or a play. Talk a walk around a park or an open air mall. Art galleries. The zoo. The aquarium. See a sports event. Go bowling." He grinned at her. "See, the options are endless."

"Obviously. What do you recommend."

"I don't know. It all depends on the company, and on a blind date you don't know much about the person."

She pointed at him. "Okay, this is a practice date and the other person is you. Where do you want to go?"

Thomas shook his head. "If we're doing this, let's do it right. You wanted a dress rehearsal. You make the judgment, based on what you know about your date—in this case, me."

"Hmm. I don't know an awful lot about you, do I?"

"I think we know each other quite well by now,

actually. You know a lot more about me than you will about the men the agency will match you up with, anyway.''

Lea grimaced and rubbed her temples. Just a mention of that agency had a migraine threatening to erupt. ''Don't remind me. Okay—with you, at least I know art galleries are out.''

''I like some art. Just not....''

''Just not horrible art.''

''That's right.''

''I don't like sports myself, so that's out.'' She shook her head. ''With that many options, it's hard to make a decision.''

''Think what you want to accomplish with the date, what kind of a message you want to send.''

''What do you mean?''

''Do you want a setting conducive to romance, or something loud and neutral that says hands off, or something to indicate your personality and your interests—or what?''

''Oh, God.''

''It's not that complicated, Lea. Just common sense.''

''Sure it's not complicated. Not compared to quantum physics or neurosurgery.''

''Hey.'' He touched the back of her hand. ''Relax. Look at it as a project.''

''Okay. How about the Aquarium?'' Lea mumbled between her fingers. ''It's somewhat romantic, but not too romantic, crowded enough to be safe for a first date with a stranger. It's possible to spend half an hour there if the guy is horrible, three hours if he's wonderful. It's both whimsical and educational. How's that for sending a message?''

"Excellent." He stood up and saluted her in good-bye. "I'll be sitting by the phone, waiting for my mysterious stranger to call."

"What?"

He winked at her as he pulled his jacket on, and his grin was downright evil. "You wanted a dress rehearsal—so let's go through the whole ritual. You pretend I'm one of the guys you got matched up with, you call me and ask me out."

"Thomas—that's just silly."

He was already out of sight, but she heard him laugh as he opened the front door. "Silly, sweetheart? Silly is our code name in this mission."

Exasperated, Lea waited a few minutes before ambling into her bedroom and curling up on her bed, phone in hand. Uruk decided to grace her with her company, stretched out on the pillows and yawned. Lea pressed the speed dial and waited for him to answer.

"Hello."

From the sound she could tell he was already in his car. "Hi, Thomas."

Pause. "Who is this, please?"

She rolled her eyes. He didn't like playacting, did he? She took a deep breath, deciding to play along. "My name is Lea. I got your name from this dating agency…"

There was laughter in Thomas's voice, but he stuck to his character. "Of course. They told me you might be in touch this week. I've been looking forward to hearing from you."

"Uh…so…" Lea wrapped Uruk's tail around her fingers until the cat swiped her hand with a paw. "Would you like to get together, maybe?"

"Absolutely. Do you have a place in mind?"

This wasn't so bad. She pressed a thumb against the pads on Uruk's paw, feeling much more optimistic about this whole thing. "I was thinking we could go to the Aquarium downtown. Ever been there?"

"No, I haven't, actually. Well—not since I was ten years old."

"Great! Tomorrow's Saturday—so shall we say two o'clock?"

"Sounds good."

"Great. See you then."

"Wait!"

She held the phone to her ear, something in his voice making her suspicious. "Yes?"

"How will I know you?"

Lea rolled over on her back and stared at the ceiling, giggling. "Oh, God, Thomas..."

"Excuse me?"

"Are you sure you weren't ever in a school play?"

"Did the agency give you my photo, perhaps?"

She tried to sober up. He seemed intent on finishing this game. "No. They didn't. How about if I stand in the piranha corner, looking really really lost and alone?"

"It's a deal. I'll be carrying a red rose."

She slapped the bed at her side with the flat of her palm. "Oh, come on, Thomas! A red rose? That's just too corny!"

"I'm sorry," he said in a wounded voice. "Would a white rose suit the lady better?"

She was in imminent danger of starting to giggle again. "Red rose. Fine. You, me and the piranhas. See you there tomorrow."

"I'll look forward to it. Good night."

"Good night. Thomas—wait!"

"Yes?"

She gnawed on her lip, wanting to say something about what a relief it was—how safe it felt—to have him helping her through it all, horrible charade or not. "You're terrific. I mean that. Thanks. I'm really grateful."

There was a moment's silence. "No problem. Good night, Lea."

Click.

She sighed as the phone landed none too gently on the nightstand, and put her head on the pillow next to Uruk's head. The cat opened an eye, blinked once and then lazily shut it again.

Would he really be carrying a red rose tomorrow?

He was.

Maybe that was the reason an innocent place like the Aquarium seemed hell of a lot more than "somewhat" romantic. Or maybe it was the company itself, Lea grudgingly admitted. She had a bit of a problem keeping things in perspective, but perhaps that was a good thing. This was supposed to be a dress rehearsal after all. It *should* feel like the real thing.

Thomas exhibited a charming trait of childish excitement over the exhibitions, and the way he turned his head with a smile, reaching out for her to share something with him, had a devastating effect on her struggling efforts to keep in mind this was all just practice for a date with someone else.

It didn't help that he grabbed her hand at the crab cages, and didn't let go until they were out in the sunlight again. Counting a snack in the cafeteria they'd been in there almost three and a half hours.

That probably put him in the wonderful rather than terrible category.

He'd forgotten about his role-playing every now and then while inside, but she could tell by the way he was looking at her as they exited the building that he was back in character. There was a teasing twinkle in his eye, and she made a face at him. It just earned her an even more teasing grin.

"That was fun," he said. "Can I drive you home?"

She opened her mouth to say yes, but there was a warning look in his eyes that told her to play along with the usual security precautions. She sighed. He was taking the game this far?

"No, I'm fine, thanks. I'll take a taxi. I have three bodyguards waiting for me at home, and five girlfriends who'll call the police if I'm not back in half an hour."

"Excellent," Thomas said blandly. He held out his hand and she took it, unprepared when he leaned closer, and by the time he straightened up again her heart was galloping like a runaway racehorse on steroids.

From a stupid *kiss on the cheek?*

How pathetic was *that?*

"We'll be in touch." She forced the words out, furious with herself for reacting this way.

Thomas grinned and made a time-out gesture. "Perfect, Lea. You pass."

"Pass what?"

"The test. Full marks. Not a step wrong anywhere. You're ready to enter the dating scene."

"I am?"

"You are. Now we just wait for that dating appointment."

Lea took a deep breath. "D day. I have it marked on my calendar in red."

D day arrived much too soon for something she'd specifically scheduled far into the future. And instead of picturing her future date with her perfect match, her head insisting on replaying her pretend date with Thomas instead. That distraction cut down on the dread—but was just as discomfiting. Not to mention that, for some reason, the red rose he'd given her at the Aquarium was now pressed between two pages in *Advanced Probability Theory*. She just couldn't bear to throw it out.

It was a memento of what she'd had to go through to find the perfect match, a husband and a father for her children, she told herself. That was all.

And now, here it was, D day, marked in huge letters in her daily planner. Thomas remembered too, and even called her at work to tell her he'd pick her up for the appointment.

The dating agency didn't look too bad, Lea thought, as they were sitting in a nicely furnished waiting room, being placated by waterfall music, but still she found herself clutching Thomas's hand like a frightened child. This wasn't so bad, she told herself again. Not at all. It could be a doctor's waiting room.

A dentist's.

Yes. This was just like going to the dentist.

In other words: an utter nightmare.

She felt Thomas's hand grip her fingers and pry them loose from his hand. "Relax, Lea. At this rate, neither of us will have any circulation left. Why are you so nervous?"

"This is a dating agency!" Lea hissed. "I never thought I would be caught dead in a place like this."

"Well, you're not dead."

Lea tightened her grasp on his hand again. "Not yet."

Thomas chuckled and squeezed her hand once in support. "You know, if you keep holding on to me like this, the staff is going to think we came in here looking for a partner to complete our threesome," he teased.

Lea ripped her hand out of his. "Seriously? This is that kind of a place?" She was half out of her seat, but Thomas got hold of her arm and held her back. She twisted her arm out of his grasp and straightened up, looking toward the door. "Maybe we shouldn't even be here. We should leave."

Thomas grabbed the back of her jacket and pulled her back until she fell into the chair. He took a magazine from the table and thrust it at her. "I was joking. This agency has an excellent reputation. Here. Read an article to take your mind off things."

"Just what I needed, another article about the etiquette of one-night stands," Lea muttered, but took the magazine and flipped through the glossy pages. "I wish they'd write one on how to meet practical, levelheaded men who want to start a family and don't worry about all this love and sex nonsense."

"'Love and sex nonsense' is the cornerstone of family, isn't it?"

"Yes. I suppose." She rolled the magazine into a tube and tapped it on her knees. "And I'm sure love will grow from a practical relationship." She looked at him. "Don't you think so?"

Thomas shrugged. "I don't know."

Lea's fist clenched around the magazine. "Well, I don't have any more time, do I?"

"I don't agree," he said calmly. "I've told you before. You're turning thirty. You've got plenty of time to start a family."

"You don't know what it's like. Everywhere. It's different for men, so I'm sure you don't have to suffer through it. People ask if I'm married or living with someone, how many children I have. Older women are the worst." She groaned. "They give me this sad look, and then they pat my shoulder and tell me there's plenty of time yet, not to worry, a lot of women are starting families in their forties these days."

"They're right. There's plenty of time. Just ignore the sad look and the shoulder pat."

"Easier said than done. Some of them try to comfort me by telling me horror stories of other women's relationships, how they were abused or cheated on, and ending with the statement that it's much better to be a happy single woman than an unhappy married woman."

"Sounds absolutely right. Those are wise women you hang out with."

"You haven't heard the tone of their voice. It says: 'Find yourself a man, you spinster! Any man! *Now!*'"

"Don't you think you're better off without that ex of yours?"

She considered that. "I suppose."

"You *suppose?*" He sent her a strange look. "Are you still in love with him?"

"No!" she protested. "Absolutely not. I wouldn't want him back, no matter what. I don't even miss him." Her voice lowered to a whisper. "But I do miss being part of a couple. It's nice. Safe…"

"But not worth it if the price is too high," he pointed out gruffly, and she nodded.

"Of course not. But this isn't just about me. It's my parents, too."

"Are they pushing?"

Lea tilted her head until her hair obscured her face. "No. Not at all. Compared to some of my friends' parents, they're incredibly patient in the wedding and grandchildren department."

"Sounds good."

"Of course, they don't know I broke up with Harry."

"What?"

She shrugged. "They live a while away, and I don't see them often. Harry came with me a couple of times in the beginning, but he's been too busy to be there in years, and, well, to be honest they never got along very well. But if Mom and Dad knew I was on my own, they'd worry about me."

"I see."

"Yes. So I postponed telling them. I thought I could present them with a fait accompli next year or so: a new man and a wedding date." She kicked at the carpeted floor. "And then—after they get over the shock of me hopping from man to man without qualms, of course—soon I could whisper to Mom that a baby quilt would come in handy in a few months." She looked up and laughed at herself, mortified to feel the hint of tears blur her sight. "Oh, Thomas, that's a pretty pathetic dream, isn't it? I really have to work on my fantasies, don't I?"

Thomas shrugged. "No, I understand your reasoning. But I don't understand what the hurry is all about.

You've got years and years before you have to worry about running out of time to have children.''

"Not quite. I'm not the only one running out of time."

He moved restlessly when she didn't elaborate. "Well, are you going to tell me why?"

"My parents. I was a late surprise to them, and I'm their only child. They're seventy years old." She exhaled noisily. "If I want my children to get to know their grandparents at all, I don't have much time."

"Are your parents healthy?"

"Yes. They're in excellent health. Now. But we don't know how long, do we? I remember my own grandmother. She was climbing mountains at seventy, but five years later she could no longer walk without aid."

"I see."

"Do you?" She looked up at him. "I don't have any brothers or sisters. When my parents are gone, my closest relatives are cousins that I haven't seen since I was ten years old."

"So you want a family."

"Yes. A family."

Thomas started to say something, but at that moment a man appeared in the doorway, beckoning them inside. "Lea Rhodes?"

"Yes. That would be me." The butterflies in her stomach started multiplying at an alarming rate, even though the young man looked relatively harmless.

"Welcome. I'm Anthony Fowler." He shook her hand and glanced at Thomas. "And you are?"

"Thomas Carlisle."

"And your relationship…?"

"I'm her dating consultant," Thomas said easily.

She could have kicked him. Why didn't he just say he was a friend? Or her brother? Anything other than 'dating consultant.' Wasn't this whole thing weird enough already?

"Her dating consultant? I see." Mr. Fowler's gaze moved between them. "How does your job differ from ours?"

"You find men, I help her judge them."

"I see." To her relief, Mr. Fowler didn't comment further on Thomas's involvement in this thing, and didn't object to him accompanying her into the room. They were seated, and the interview began.

It wasn't long. To Lea's surprise it wasn't excruciating either. Not a single fingernail was pulled. After only ten minutes, Mr. Fowler opened a drawer and dug up a stack of paper to place in front of her. "These are personality tests and interest charts—they ask for all sorts of information about you. If you'd fill them out, using the enclosed computer score sheet, it will help us find a match."

"Do I do this now?" she said, looking at the huge stack.

"You can take it home and bring it back tomorrow if you like."

"Good. I'll do that. Then what happens?"

"We feed your information into the computer. It finds several suitable matches. We interview them, and estimate how well the computer has matched you. Then, when we've found a couple of candidates, we'll be in touch and you'll receive information about them, including their names and phone numbers. After that— it's up to you. You can contact them if you want to. Or not."

"They get my number?" Lea interrupted.

Mr. Fowler shook his head. "No. Only the women get phone numbers. That's one of our security precautions. You call them, and if everything goes well, you arrange to meet. If things don't work out, you come back to us, and we'll find other matches."

Lea took a deep breath. "So, now I just wait for you to get back to me, and then I just call them?"

"Yes."

Okay. At least she had a few days of reprieve.

Thomas put his arm around her shoulders when they were outside on the pavement and gave her a squeeze, pushing all the air out of her lungs. "See? That wasn't so bad. There was no need for you to stay up all night worrying."

"How did you know…?"

He touched her face, his thumb moving over her cheekbone. Again, for no reason at all, she had trouble breathing. Maybe she was developing asthma. "Circles under your eyes."

She grimaced. "Great. Well, it's over, and I've got a few days to get rid of the circles before I have to impress a guy. And I really think something might come out of this. They sound very professional."

"Yes. I did a bit of research on them. Their reputation is excellent. They're expensive, but reputed to be worth it."

Lea hefted the pile of paper. "Will you help me go through the paperwork?"

Thomas shook his head. "Probably not a good idea. Those are personality tests—hardly something to consult someone else about. You wouldn't get valid results that way."

"You're right," she said, reluctant to let him just

leave. She didn't want to be alone, not right now with the prospect of being electronically matched to a stranger somewhere. "But at least let me cook for you tonight. It's almost dinnertime, and I owe you."

"Thanks, I'd like to have dinner with you. But you don't owe me anything."

"I do owe you."

"You're paying me, remember?" he pointed out dryly.

"Since you brought that up..."

"Uh, oh."

"Yes. You still haven't cashed the check I gave you," she accused. "I checked my bank."

He wasn't very good at hiding his grin. "Haven't been to the bank yet."

"It's yours. I'm certainly making you work hard enough for it. If you don't cash the check yourself, I will find another way to get the money to you." She smiled sweetly at him, the perfect attack strategy coming to her in a flash of brilliant inspiration. "I know— I'll use the money to buy you a sculpture."

"I'll cash the check," Thomas said hurriedly with a crooked grin. "I promise. Please—no horrible works of art."

An hour later, Thomas was making the salad and stirring the sauce, as Lea had completely forgotten about it herself in the pleasure of going through the tests. They seemed to appeal to her statistician's mind, and although she voiced quite a few reservations about the validity of the calculations they would make, on the whole she seemed to approve. She'd taken one look at them while waiting for the oven to warm—and he'd taken over the cooking when the water boiled over and she didn't even notice.

"You know, a lot of these questions actually make sense," she mused.

"Does that surprise you?"

"Yeah. I had a friend who was a psych major, and she put me through all sorts of personality questionnaires. They had the silliest questions."

"All the better to drag all those deep dark secrets out from the bottom of your soul."

"But this really makes sense. I mean, it asks about feelings toward family, children, ethical issues, political views. It looks like I won't even have to ask them about the children's issues, the details will be in their basic information. I probably won't even get any matches with men who don't want children. I'm impressed."

"Good." He started setting the table, which woke her up. She scrambled to gather the papers together, looking guilt-stricken.

"I'm sorry—I was supposed to be in the middle of cooking dinner! I forgot." She put the stack out of the way and peered into the oven. "You did that?"

"Yeah. It was no problem. Everything's ready. We just have to set the table."

"You can cook, eh?"

"Of course." He winked at her. "You don't become a confirmed bachelor and a *player* without learning your way around the kitchen."

She smiled, and as usual, it did something to his gut. This time, it might be because she'd just poked it with a finger. "Of course. And a diet of take-out and junk food would do nasty things to that physique of yours and make it harder to attract the babes."

"Are you saying women would just want me for my body?" he asked in mock indignation. "What about my personality, my intelligence, my irresistible charm?"

"Not to mention your ego. Sit down, the least I can do is set the table."

He leaned against the wall with his arms crossed and watched her reach up into the cupboards for plates and glasses. "Is that another thing your man should lack, an ego?"

"I'm looking for a family man, not a serial dater," she said. "If ego plays into that, then yes, I'm looking for someone who doesn't have a colossal ego."

Thomas started pulling his stool out from under the small table, but she pointed behind him. "There's a proper chair there. I brought it in from the bedroom."

"For me?" He grinned at her. "Thoughtful of you."

"Well, in case our plan works, I suppose I should get used to having to account for having a man around," she muttered.

So he just keeping someone else's seat warm, was he? That wasn't a very comfortable thought. "You don't sound very enthusiastic about it."

She shrugged. "It'll take some getting used to."

"I've been thinking," Thomas said as they sat down on the table. "I don't think it's smart to aim for finding a husband right away, when you've only had one relationship."

"What do you mean?" She sampled his cooking, which was little more than random things from her fridge thrown on top of the fish, with lots of cheese on top. "Mmm. This is good, Thomas! This is much better than what I had in mind."

Thomas ignored her compliment, as he had more

important things to say. He had a feeling she was about to make a terrible mistake. "You may not know what you're missing. You should sow your wild oats a bit before settling down."

"Sow my wild oats?" She put her fork down to better concentrate on staring at him. "Thomas, I'm a woman. I don't have any *oats* to sow."

"You know what I mean. You should at least have one last fling before settling down."

"A fling?" she repeated suspiciously. "I don't have flings."

"What? Never?"

"You mean like a one-night stand with a complete stranger? No. No way."

"Not a one-night stand with a stranger. Just a fling with someone you're attracted to—without attaching forever after, babies and a fiftieth wedding anniversary to the package."

Her eyes narrowed. "Can't I have a fling with someone I'm attracted to—and attach the whole package too?"

"Sure. If you find one."

"Good. Let's just work on that, then."

"Okay. You're the boss. But I still think a fling is just what you need."

Interesting suggestion, Tom, his conscience taunted him. *And just who did you have in mind for her 'last fling'?*

Shut up, he told himself.

CHAPTER SIX

THREE sheets of paper.

Three men. Adrian, Paul and Roger. Their vital statistics, their hobbies and interests, and a short biography. All she had to do was pick up the phone and call one of them.

She grabbed the phone and called Thomas.

"I got it," she said breathlessly as soon as he picked up the phone. She'd learned that there wasn't any need to introduce herself, he always recognized her voice instantly.

"Good. You got it. Now, what exactly did you get?"

"The guys!" She cleared her throat, appalled at the way she sounded. Next she'd start giggling like a schoolgirl. "I mean—they found me some matches." That was better. A calm and professional voice. "The agency. I have their information right here."

"I see."

"Can you come over after work? I'll feed you, promise."

"What do you need me for?"

"Work," she said succinctly. "Or are you backing out on me?"

There was a silence that managed to scare her. Was he backing out on her? It wouldn't be surprising. There was nothing really in this for him—except perhaps the friendship that had formed between them. Sure, she was paying him, but he wasn't doing this for the money.

But thinking about it, she wasn't sure she'd be doing this on her own. Having someone to talk to, someone to roll his eyes over her nerves, was reassuring.

"Sure. I'll come over. Not sure what good I'm going to do, but I'll be there. Do I get to cook again?"

"No. We'll order pizza. How's that?"

"Sounds good. I'll try to be there by seven, okay?"

Thomas had memorized all three men's vital statistics after Lea had read them to him six times. She couldn't decide which one of them to contact first, and he refused to give his opinion and influence her choice. She wasn't pleased.

"Okay, how about this: We each write down their names, in the order of preference, and then exchange notes."

He shrugged. His stomach was beginning to gently remind him they'd been promised pizza. "Okay. Sure. But then you call the one you choose, okay?"

She was jotting down the name and didn't answer. He wrote his own choice down, and she ripped it out of his hand as soon as he was done, tossing her own note on his chest. They'd chosen the same guy.

"Paul, huh?" she said. "He's at the top of both of our lists. Why him?"

"His letter sounded like he was a down to earth, regular guy."

"Good. I'll call him." She glanced toward the phone. "I guess I should do it now, or I might lose my nerve."

Thomas stood up. "Great." He bent down to kiss her cheek. "Good luck. I know you'll charm him."

When he turned around to leave he didn't get far

because she was hanging on to his sleeve. "Where do you think you're going?" she asked indignantly.

"Into the kitchen to order pizza on my cell phone. I'm giving you privacy to chat with Paul."

She moved her hand to his wrist and got a secure hold on him. "You're not leaving me alone to face this."

He stared at her for a moment, then pulled his cell phone out of his pocket and grabbed the piece of paper she had clenched in her fists. He started punching in the digits. She slammed her hand over his phone. "What are you doing?" she shrieked.

"Calling Paul."

"You're not talking to him!"

He rolled his eyes. "I wasn't going to talk to him. He'd think I'm gay or something. I'm calling him, then I'm handing you the phone so you can get this over with. You know that thinking about it just gets you into trouble."

She took the phone from him and jammed it back into his pocket. "Just stay here. You don't even have to listen. In fact, it's better if you don't listen. I just need you to be here in case of…"

"In case of what?"

"An emergency."

"What sort of an emergency might that be? I'm not coaching you through a telephone call, Lea. Besides, I'm just as lost as you are. I've never done this either."

Her hold on his wrist was tight enough to nearly cut off blood circulation. "Stay with me, at least. I mean, if I start to stutter, or say something terribly stupid, you grab the phone away from me and hang up, okay? And if I faint, you throw cold water on me. You know. Just an emergency backup."

He couldn't resist her when she asked him for a favor looking at him with need in her eyes. He didn't even try. He allowed her to pull him to the living room sofa. She left him there, and fetched the telephone, then sat so close she was practically in his lap.

"Okay, best to just do it, right? Get it over with?"

"Right."

Despite her apparent nerves, Lea was charming on the phone, and the man at the other end seemed to appreciate it. He heard only the low murmur of his voice as Lea had the phone pressed to her ear, her knuckles white, but her tension didn't show at all in her voice. He was rather impressed.

"Friday, six o'clock. Yes, I know the place. That's great. I'll look forward to it."

Her finishing words brought him out of his reverie. Lea was hanging up, her cheeks red. She threw her arms around him and hugged him. "I did it! I have a date. Friday. He sounds okay. I don't think he's an ax murderer or anything."

"Good. Great. Where are you going? The Aquarium?"

"No—actually, he suggested the place. A restaurant that's just across the street from the dating agency. So it's a neutral place, but we've both been to that street. Not a bad idea."

"Okay." Good. He didn't have much enthusiasm for traipsing around the Aquarium again, this time watching Lea holding hands with some other guy. It would feel very…wrong.

"Oh boy." She practically bounced up and down. "I have a date. A real date with a man who's been specifically matched to me. And I have you to thank for it."

"Not really."

She didn't hear, but her bouncing slowed down until she was sitting on the edge of the sofa, her hands clenching the cushions by her thighs. "Oh, God. I have a date."

"It'll be okay, don't worry."

"You don't understand. It's on Friday. I only have two days."

"You're going on a date. How much can you possibly need to prepare?"

How could an intelligent man ask such a stupid question?

There were a thousand decisions to be made. What clothes to wear, what perfume, style of makeup, high, higher or highest heels.

Then there was a strategy to be determined. There'd been an article, "Impress Your Date", that she "hadn't read" in that women's magazine she'd "barely glanced at," and she remembered every excruciating detail.

Coy or flirt? Mysterious or open? Talkative or quiet?

Be yourself, yes—but what sides of yourself to display? Statistics and calculations were so much easier than this.

"Dating is such a hassle," she said with a sigh, but Thomas was still staring at her as if he didn't understand at all what the problem was. Men. They had it so easy. Especially guys like him. She glared at him.

"What did I do now?" he asked, eyebrows raised and hands lifted in a gesture of complete innocence. She snorted, thinking about the scores of women he dated.

"When was your last date, Thomas?"

"That would have been our double date with your Footsie and my Bubble Gum."

"It was cruel of us to dump Beth like that," she said.

Thomas shrugged. "Don't worry about it. I called her the next day and apologized again. She was fine. She even had plans to see James again."

"You haven't been out with anyone since then?"

"I've been busy."

"Oh," she muttered. "Right. I'm cramping your style, aren't I?"

"Don't worry about my style. Tell me about that date. Is he picking you up?"

"No, we're meeting there. That's one of the safety tips the agency suggested."

"Right. And on the subject of safety tips—I've been meaning to talk to you about something: you should know better than to get into a car with strange men you've just met."

"Of course! I'd never..." She closed her mouth as the reason for his stern frown became clear. "Oh."

"Yes."

"Well, that was different. It was you."

"You didn't know me."

She grinned at him. "Well, I'm still extremely happy that I did get into the car with you. I couldn't have come this far without you. I would probably still be hiding in the bathtub, trying to scrub James off my legs."

Thomas looked down at her legs. She could almost feel his gaze as a physical touch. She cleared her throat. "Would you do something for me?"

He took a long time looking back up into her face. "Yes?"

"Can we go on a practice date?"

"We already did that."

"Can we go on another one?"

"Are you kidding?"

"No. I'd feel better if we went to that restaurant. Scouted it out. You know."

Thomas shrugged. "Sure. No problem. Tomorrow evening, then?"

"Why not now? Instead of pizza. I'll ring and see if they have a table tonight."

They'd just entered the restaurant when a feminine voice called Thomas's name. Lea braced herself to meet one of his girlfriends, when someone wound her arms around *her* neck.

She'd smelled that perfume before.

"You're still together!" Beth was beaming when she drew back and attacked Thomas with an equally enthusiastic hug. "That's wonderful. I've thought about you every now and then."

Lea moved closer to Thomas and put her arm around his waist. It wouldn't do to let Beth know that her sacrifice had been less than worth it. "Yes. We're still together." She felt Thomas's arm come around her and cursed silently. She still had trouble breathing when he touched her, damn it. She tried to clear her head and focus her attention on Beth. "I heard you and James hit it off?"

"Well, no. Not really. I met him a couple of times, but he's not my type. But that's okay." She smiled at Thomas. "To tell you the truth, you did seem a bit...old for me, anyway."

"Aw, honey," Lea teased, looking up at Thomas's

face. "Don't worry. I don't think you're over the hill at all."

Thomas growled down at her.

Lea chuckled as Beth left the restaurant with her date. "That was interesting. How does it feel to be over the hill, grandpa?"

Thomas squeezed her shoulder hard in punishment. "Let's go inside grandma, and order our prunes."

Lea took a deep breath when they'd been seated. "Friday I'll be here on a blind date with someone I'm meeting through a dating agency. Unbelievable."

"It'll be fine, Lea. I mean—we've been on dates of sorts. A man and a woman, together at a restaurant. It's pretty much like what you'll be doing on Friday. Not such a big deal."

Lea shook her head. "It's not the same at all. I'm not nervous at all when I'm out with you. Because there aren't any expectations or unresolved issues. Neither of us is on trial. I don't have to impress you, and I don't have to imagine what you're like in bed."

Thomas seemed to choke on something, but they hadn't even been served their drinks yet.

"Excuse me?"

"That's what the articles say. Visualize intimate situations before they arise."

"And women actually do that?"

"I don't know. Do men?"

He seemed reluctant to answer and developed a sudden interest in the candle at the center of the table, which was an excellent reply in itself.

"Hmm. Of course they do. No surprise there. Anyway, the article recommended that as a shortcut way of deciding how you really felt about a man."

"Have you put that theory to the test?"

Did random images flashing through her brain count? Yes, they probably did. The lighting was dim. He wouldn't see her blush, so she could answer nonchalantly. "Sure. No harm in thoughts, is there?"

"And does this work?"

"Kind of. I knew James was out even before his foot started crawling up my leg."

"So, your man does not only have to fulfill your expectations for suitability, he also has to pass your mental sex test?"

"Yep."

Thomas shook his head and picked up the menu. "Women. You're weird. At least I don't have to get inside your head to assist with the fantasies."

That's what you think, Lea almost said.

"How do I look?" Lea reminded him of a contortionist as she twisted and turned in front of the mirror in an attempt to see herself from all angles. "Thomas? How do I look?"

What an archetypal woman's question. One that could bring a man to his knees again and again, begging for mercy. And even so, the answer never mattered, did it? What a woman saw in the mirror was never what her man saw.

Her man? Thomas shook his head, confused. He hadn't been thinking about himself as her man, had he?

"Well?" she asked again, impatient when he hadn't answered. "Do I look okay?"

"You look terrific, Lea," he said, and he meant it. "You look lovely. If you'd just stop biting your lip and frowning, I'll update my verdict to gorgeous."

She glared at him in the mirror and started messing with her hair. He grabbed her hands and stilled them, meeting her nervous gaze in the mirror. "Don't. Your hair is perfect."

"It's not."

"It is," he insisted. "Everything's perfect. You look gorgeous. I mean it. Stop worrying."

She yanked her hands free and stared into the mirror with renewed anxiety. "Do I look too…something?"

"Too what?"

She shrugged, stealing a strand of hair to wrap nervously around her fingers. The mirror frowned back at them, but she still looked lovely. "You know. Like I put too much effort into it. Like I'm trying too hard. Or something. Anything that will put him off?"

Thomas groaned and shoved a hand through his hair in a defeated gesture. "I don't believe this. Is this what you women go through before every single date?"

"Well, in my limited experience: yes."

"Sympathies."

"Thank you."

"I'm glad I didn't have a sister growing up. Going through this, even vicariously, would have been torture."

"Didn't you say you had a stepsister? The one who set you up?"

"Yes. But she's a late addition to the family. My father married her mother just a couple of years ago. We're friends, but not really brother and sister."

Lea nodded and her forehead collapsed into a frown again. "Maybe I shouldn't wear red. Too flamboyant. Isn't it?"

"No. You look wonderful in red. Now, step away from that mirror and try to relax. We've still got ten minutes before we have to leave."

"Ten minutes? I could change in ten minutes. And

redo my hair. And if I'm not wearing red, I need to redo some of my makeup.''

Lea was probably mentally standing in her bedroom, closet door almost ripped off the hinges, when she realized she was still in the hallway, held in a vise. He watched her glance down at her arm where he'd curled a hand around her upper arm. Tight.

''Thomas?''

''You're not changing clothes, Lea. You're perfect just the way you are. Don't mess with anything.''

She took a deep breath and looked up into his eyes. ''Are you sure?''

''Trust me,'' he said, his voice soft. ''That guy won't believe his luck.''

''Aw. Sweet.'' She hadn't put on her heels yet, so she stood on tiptoe to kiss his cheek. His blood pressure doubled. ''Thanks. You're a terrific self-esteem booster.''

''You're welcome.''

''But what if he's terrible?'' she asked, fidgeting again. ''What if he's into footsie, like James?''

''I'll be right there, remember? If he gives you even hint of a trouble, I'll rescue you, just like last time.''

''Promise?''

She looked so cute, staring anxiously up at him with a worried frown between her brows, that he could see himself charging in, sweeping her up and vanishing into the night with her. ''I promise.''

''I'm so nervous, Thomas.''

''Don't be.''

''Easy for you to say.''

''Relax, Lea.''

''I can't. It's a physical impossibility. I think my entire system is flooded with adrenaline.''

"Were you this nervous for your date with Mr. Footsie?"

"No. He was just a practice date. I went into that one with no expectations. In fact, I went into it with a blind date expectations, and it wasn't even as bad as I was afraid it might be."

"What's the problem now? Do you have higher expectations?"

"Yeah. You picked this one."

Thomas groaned. "Don't have this much faith in me, Lea. All I did was choose some of your requirements to have fed into a computer that spit out names for you."

"You approved him, also."

"That means you can blame me if things go wrong. That does not mean this is your one and only chance at impressing your future husband and father of your children."

"I know. I'm sorry. I'm acting like a child."

"It'll be okay. I'll be right there. You can see me, I can see you. All you have to do is give me a sign, and I run right over and rescue you."

She laughed. "Are you going to whisk me off my feet, kiss me until my toes curl and carry me out to your car?"

Not a bad idea. The image thundered through his mind, and left tingles in its aftermath. Not a bad idea at all—but he didn't think Lea would feel the same way. "What are you talking about?"

She shook her head. "Nothing. That was the rumor James fed to my brother-in-law, that you'd swept me off my feet—literally—and ravished me on the spot. He seems to have a wild imagination."

"It's an interesting idea. I'll be sure to keep that in mind if the occasion arises."

She grinned, taking his words as a joke, completely oblivious to the undercurrents that were threatening to drown him. No wonder she needed his assistance, he grumbled silently. She really didn't have a clue on how to read men.

"Thanks, Thomas. I really am appreciative. You know that, don't you?" She didn't wait for an answer, but hugged him, pressing a quick kiss on his cheek. He felt its impact deep in his gut. "For a serial dater, you're a nice guy." She winked. "But then I'm not dating you, thank God."

"Right," he muttered. "You're dating Paul Cameron."

"Yeah. I've got some last minute questions."

"Fire away."

"Okay, I'm going on a date with a total stranger. At the end of the evening…I can't be expected to kiss him, or am I?"

"You're not *expected* to do anything you don't want to."

"What's the norm? What do most people do?"

"You're not most people, Lea. You're you."

Her brows drew together. "Stop the self-help crap. I just want to get through this, taking the middle of the road. Kiss or no kiss?"

He gave up. She wanted rules, he'd give her rules. "No kiss."

She looked relieved for a fraction of a microsecond, then worry took over again. "You're sure about that?" She pushed a finger into his chest. "You don't kiss on first dates?"

"We're not talking about me. We're talking about

you, and since you're already having a nervous break-down over this, we're deciding that you're not doing any kissing.''

She wasn't looking anywhere close to convinced. ''What is he expecting? What do *you* expect on a first date?''

''Nothing.''

''Really?''

''Really. No expectations—no disappointments, no misunderstanding, no regrets. Not to mention, room for spontaneity if the circumstances are favorable.''

The anxious look was back on her face. ''Are you sure? Because there was this article, it said you should kiss on first date, but maximum two seconds, and no— you know, tongue.''

Thomas looked up at the ceiling and took a deep breath. ''Lea, sometimes you sound sixteen. Two sec-onds and no 'you know' tongue?''

Now she looked guilty, although he couldn't begin to guess why that particular emotion should surface. ''The article said that. It wasn't a teen magazine. But you're right. I'm not sixteen, dammit, I shouldn't be so insecure.'' Her hands were in her hair again, tugging at it in frustration. She started pacing back and forth. ''Oh, God, Thomas, what a mess. I shouldn't do this. I'm being stupid, aren't I? This is such a mess. Maybe I should just—''

''Lea...'' He grabbed her wrist as her frantic pacing brought her close. ''Relax.''

''Why did you agree to do this, Thomas? It's ridic-ulous. I'm asking you how I should kiss someone, for God's sake. I suppose I should be grateful you haven't called men in white coats to come get me yet...''

Her face was flushed, her eyes wide and green, and

her hands cold with anxiety. He opened his mouth, intending to say something calming and constructive, something to calm her down. But then all of a sudden his lips were on hers. He hadn't planned it, hadn't had any idea it was about to happen until his hands were in her hair, tilting her head up. It was quick, surprisingly heated, and when it was over it felt like the mistake it had been.

Still, with a kind of a stubborn satisfaction, he refused to regret it. It had been hanging in the air between them since the evening they'd first met. Now it was out of the way.

Lea was silent for a small eternity. He didn't speak either, just stared back at her startled face. She took a deep breath and touched her lips with a finger. It was such a telling, unconscious gesture that he had to restrain himself to keep from touching her again. Then she raised her eyebrows in question.

"Interesting, Thomas. Is that how I should kiss him?" she asked quietly.

He buried his hands in his pockets and stared her down. Attack was the best defense, wasn't it? But her lips sure were soft. And she'd been just as involved as he'd been. Of course, she had her own agenda. She'd been *practicing,* damn it. "No. I already told you: no kiss. That's how you don't kiss him."

Lea's gaze was unflinching. "I see. You did that to show me what not to do?"

"No, I did it to shut you up and calm your nerves."

She shook her head slightly, her eyes still dark and deep and not letting him off the hook. "Funny, it doesn't seem to have calmed my nerves."

Thomas shrugged. "Well, I did my best. It did shut you up for about ten seconds."

She scowled at him, and he reached out and ran his thumb over the crease between her eyes, relieved to have an opening to end this discussion. "If you keep frowning this much before every date, you're going to get some serious wrinkles during our mission," he teased.

She blanched and vanished to the bathroom.

"Lea!" he called after her. "I was teasing you. You don't have wrinkles."

"I'm just a few weeks away from turning thirty," she called back. "Wrinkles are waiting to pounce on me. You don't make wrinkle jokes to a woman who's about to turn thirty. It might just push her over the edge."

He shuffled to the bathroom and leaned against the open door. "I'm sorry. I told you: no sister when I was growing up."

Lea was leaning toward the mirror and rubbing some sort of cream between her eyes. She was looking even more flustered than before.

"That gooey stuff is going to stop wrinkles from appearing?" he asked.

"Probably not," she muttered, twisting the cap back on the bottle. "Somewhere, someone is sitting in a penthouse office, cackling madly and bathing in the billions he made by fooling wrinkle-fearing women the world over."

"Wrinkles aren't that bad. I have some."

She glanced at him in a way that would have shown wrinkles if she'd had any. "Yes. You have some around your eyes that deepen when you laugh, and they only make you look mature and attractive. Men! It's not fair. God is definitely not a woman, or this would be very much a different world."

Thomas dug in his pocket for his car keys. He'd put his jacket on half an hour ago, when she'd for the third time decided *now* she was ready. "Shall we save the theology discussion for later and get going?"

Lea made Thomas drop her off in front of the restaurant, with strict instructions to circle the block and then park a distance away so her date wouldn't know they were together. He rolled his eyes a bit, but complied, leaving her standing on the steps of the restaurant, feeling alone and lost. Abandoned.

"Idiot," she muttered to herself and started up the stairs. Almost thirty years old and she'd hired a chaperone for her date. It was pathetic. Then again, it was smart, wasn't it? You never knew these days. A bodyguard wasn't a bad idea.

She was early, and was relieved to find that Paul was not, and she could sit down at their table and compose herself. She glanced out the window, on the lookout, until she realized she was scouting for Thomas, since she only had a vague idea of what Paul looked like.

Thomas took his time arriving, and her frazzled nerves started complaining. He wouldn't dump her, would he? After all their preparations? He *had* to get here before Paul did.

"Lea?"

He was here.

Both of them.

Lea shook Paul's hand, giving him her very best smile. He had a warm handshake, a nice smile, and immediately passed the first impressions test.

As he sat down, she glared at Thomas who'd sat

down at his own table and was currently hiding behind a menu. How dare he be late when she needed him?

Thomas was bored.

Like true professionals, they'd researched the layout of the restaurant the other night, and selected the perfect tables for this mission. His single table was in the exact spot so that he could see Lea, see as much of her date as possible without him noticing, and he was even close enough so that he might be able to hear some of the conversation. It was perfect.

And he felt like a perfect idiot. For one thing, he'd never in his life gone out to dinner alone before, let alone in a restaurant like this one, which seemed to be all about couples. Already he'd received a few pitying glances, and he didn't like it one bit.

There wasn't much for him to do, either. Despite Lea's nerves, she passed every test with flying colors— if there had been a test in the first place. She was charming, funny, and seemed to get along great with her date. Who also passed all tests, Thomas acknowledged grudgingly. He was polite and attentive. There wasn't a single warning sign. Which was good, he reminded himself. This was good.

He went through the eating ritual, trying to pace himself to them, which was a challenge, given that their eating was interrupted by conversation, and his was not. He should have brought a newspaper or something. A blow-up doll to talk to. A handheld computer game. Anything.

He'd just finished ordering dessert when he noticed Lea trying to catch his eye without Paul noticing. He raised an eyebrow in question and she gestured toward the hallway leading to the rest rooms. He stood up and walked to there. A few minutes later, Lea swept majestically past him and into one of the three doors marked as the ladies' room without giving him a second glance.

Now what? Thomas hesitated. She didn't really expect him to enter the ladies' room, did she?

Lea's hand appeared from the crack between the door and the jamb, and grabbed the front of his shirt. His buttons nearly popped as she dragged him inside and slammed the door behind him.

Obviously, she did.

He was relieved to find himself in a tiny cubicle, instead of a huge common room. Someone might have seen him enter, and someone might see him leave, but at least nobody would shriek at finding him inside.

Except Lea, possibly.

"Hmm," he muttered, trying to shift so the door handle didn't press into his back. "Wonder if they designed this room as a practice place for Mile High Club prospectives?"

"What?"

"Nothing. How's it going? What's so urgent that you dragged me in here?"

"I forgot," she whispered. "Money issues. What about paying? What's the standard? Dutch? This kind of a date—that seems most fair, but I don't want to insult him. What do I do?"

Thomas shrugged. "I don't know. I always pay."

"Because you want to, or because it's expected?"

"A little of both, I suppose."

"Do your dates offer to pay?"

"Sometimes. Especially on a first date, yes."

"And you don't let them?"

"Generally not, no. Unless they're really insistent, of course."

"Do they insist? How forcefully? How much is too much, how little is too little?"

"Lea!" He grabbed her arms and cursed. "I swear, you're one of the most neurotic women that I know. Lightning won't strike you down if you don't do everything absolutely correct."

"Thomas, save the pep talk for later," she snarled. "We're getting to the dessert, I don't have much time. What do I do?"

"Okay, offer to pay your share. If he objects, you can insist if you want to, but don't take it too far."

"Yeah." She rested her forehead on his shoulder and sighed. "Sounds logical. We don't want to have a fistfight over the bill, do we?"

"No." He patted her back. "Straighten up, lady. This will all work out fine. He seems like a nice enough guy."

"Yeah," she said. "He's nice. Really nice. I like him."

"Good." He cupped her pale face in his palm and tapped her lower lip with his thumb. "Don't bite your lip. Smile. You're gorgeous. I hope that guy appreciates the privilege of being out with you."

Her smile was faint, but it did emerge. "Thanks. You're really nice too, Thomas."

"You bet I am. Now, go back there and keep dazzling him."

She got two steps away before she turned around. He shook his head in warning. "Don't, Lea. You're doing fine. Go charm him."

She hesitated, then smiled and turned around.

Thomas clenched his jaw. Lucky Paul.

*   *   *

Lea said goodbye to Paul at the restaurant, explaining that a friend would pick her up. More security precautions, she explained with a grimace and Paul nodded, saying he understood perfectly. She stared after him as he crossed the road to his car, and drove away.

Everything had gone great.

It would have been a perfect date, had not Thomas been sitting there, just across the room, meeting her eyes every time she looked. She'd thought it would make her feel safe, but instead it made her feel… nervous. He was watching her closely as he'd promised, she couldn't complain about that. And it was unnerving. It reminded her of that shut-up-and-calmdown kiss he'd given her. That little thing wasn't helping her resolution to keep him on the mentor shelf. It wouldn't help those random flashes of fantasy that weren't letting up.

Thomas was not one of her candidates, she sternly reminded her brain. He was *not*.

"Is the coast clear?" a voice asked close to her ear, startling her almost to the level of whacking him with her purse.

"Yes. He's gone."

Thomas put his arm around her shoulders and squeezed. "Congratulations. You survived your first date. How was it?"

"Not bad," she said. "Quite good, actually. But then you know that. You were there."

"It looked like you got along fine. Did you have a nice time?"

"Yeah. He's a nice guy. We had a nice time together."

Even to her own ears she sounded very unenthusiastic. The look on Thomas' face indicated he noticed.

"Interested?"

"I think so. Yes, I think he probably is."

"Of course *he* is," Thomas said impatiently. "What
man wouldn't be? I meant you. How about you?"

"Oh. Yes. I think I'm interested. He's so nice."

"You're saying 'nice' an awful lot, Lea."

"Well, it's true. He's nice."

Thomas pulled her with him toward the exit. "Let's
go. Think you might have something there?"

"Yeah. Could be. Maybe."

"Meeting him again?"

Lea turned her head to look at him, confused at the
brusque tone of his voice. Hadn't he liked Paul? Had
he seen something she'd missed? "Yes. Tuesday evening. We're going to a museum."

"Cool." He opened the car door for her and she got
in. He hadn't liked Paul, that much was sure. Her heart
sank. Had she misjudged the man? Thomas had to have
seen something she hadn't, but why wasn't he sharing?

As soon as Thomas had gotten into the driver's seat,
she pounced. "You didn't like him, did you?"

"Sure. I don't have any problems with him."

"Thomas, be honest with me. What do your instincts
tell you? Is he trouble?"

Thomas rubbed his forehead with the back of his
hand, then started the car. "Honestly, Lea—I don't see
any problems with him. He may be your dream man."

"Honest?" Lea asked. His tone seemed forced.

"Yes. So, can I say my job here is done and ride
off into the sunset?"

"No." Absolutely not. Especially if he wasn't sure
Paul was okay, and she wasn't convinced yet. "Oh, no.

I still need you, Thomas. You'll come to the museum, won't you? Just hang around somewhere in the immediate vicinity.''

"Why? The ice is broken, he's a nice guy...what's the problem?''

"You're my security blanket.''

Thomas gave a sound that was half groan, half laugh. "Warm and fuzzy?''

"A necessary item in battling the cruel and evil world.''

"Lea...''

"Please?''

Thomas' lips pressed together for a few seconds. Then he shook his head. "Okay, fine. I'll do it. But don't count on me being there forever.''

"Of course not. Don't worry. Someday I've got to stand on my own feet. I know.''

Thomas groaned. "Yes. And someday, I've got to learn how to say no to pretty women.''

CHAPTER SEVEN

AS HE watched Lea get ready for her fourth date with Paul—her first unchaperoned date—answering her million questions a minute without getting any indication that she was paying any attention to his answers, Thomas felt as if he was about to abandon his baby for the first time.

Of course, he didn't have a baby—but he could imagine that the feeling of unease, worry and anxiety had to be similar to what a parent would feel.

And unlike parents leaving their infant home with a baby-sitter, he wouldn't be able to call every ten minutes to check up on his "baby," would he? No, he'd have to wait until tomorrow to call her and hear how it had gone.

This felt all wrong.

Lea was nervous too. He could see it in her body language, although she kept insisting she was fine.

"You're not fine," he said at last. "Lea, you're practically trembling with nerves. Why? You've met him a few times before, you're getting along great. I haven't intervened in any way, just spied on you from afar. You haven't needed me at all. Why is it such a problem for you to go on this date without me?"

"It's not the alone bit that worries me."

Of course not. Why had he instantly assumed it was his protection that she'd miss? She didn't need him. Not any more. "Then what?" he asked. "Tell me. Talking about it helps."

She grinned at him. "Does it, Dr. Carlisle?"

Thomas faked an Austrian accent and patted the couch. "Come here, Miss Rhodes. Tell me your problems."

Lea didn't sit down. Instead she paced the floor for a few minutes, before apparently coming to a decision. She stopped and wrung her hands, her head tilted down to stare into the carpet.

"Okay: this is my problem." She took a breath so deep it seemed to drain all the air from the room. "You see—I think it may be time."

Thomas glanced at his watch. "Time for what?"

"To kiss," she whispered. "I think it may be time to…kiss him tonight." Her voice was as unenthusiastic as it could possibly be. Her face looked like she were contemplating chewing on a lemon for dinner.

He didn't find it hard to imagine the sour taste himself. The very idea turned his stomach. Was she doing the right thing? Were *they* doing the right thing? He looked at her pale face, and shook his head. He got to his feet and walked closer to her.

"Lea, you need to look in a mirror, right now."

She glanced at him in surprise, and he put his hands on her shoulders and marched her to the hallway mirror. "Look."

She looked. He met her eyes in the mirror. They were dark, the brows drawn together, and her teeth were worrying her lip again. Her shoulders were bundled in knots under his hands. He rubbed at the tense muscles with his thumbs and shook his head.

"Look at yourself. You look terrified, practically nauseous. If you feel like that about kissing him, he's definitely not someone you want to make a baby with."

"No. It's not like that, Thomas. I really like Paul. He's really nice."

"Really?"

"Yes. I should want to…" she said, as if trying to convince herself. "It wouldn't be…terrible, or anything. I mean, he's nice, fun, he's even good-looking. I *like* him. There's nothing *wrong* with him."

She turned around to face him and briefly rested her forehead on his shoulder. She did that a lot, he realized. It made him want to envelop her in a tight hug, and not let her wander off on a date with another man. Damn.

"Did he flunk your mental sex test?"

"Not…exactly."

He held his breath, hating the idea of Paul passing that ridiculous test of hers. "What do you mean?"

"He's… Oh, it's hard to explain. I haven't really done that test, since just the idea of kissing is…scary. I don't know why. So far he seems perfect for me. I should *want* to kiss him, Thomas."

Thomas groaned. "What's the problem, then?"

"I don't know. It just doesn't feel right. It's probably just beginner's nerves. Don't you think so? I'll be fine when it's over and done with. Right?"

"I'm not being paid nearly enough for this job," he muttered. "You need a therapist, not a dating consultant." He was feeling irritated, and denial wasn't working. He wasn't all noble and self-sacrificing. He didn't have her best interests at heart. He didn't at all like the idea of her kissing Paul Cameron. Not one bit.

She'd pulled away from him, but was still standing so close. He looked over her shoulder to distract himself, but that wasn't any better, because there was the mirror and her hair looked so lovely, falling down her back, that he could barely restrain himself from burying his hands in it. "What do you think?" she asked. "Should we kiss tonight?"

He sighed and tore his gaze away from the mirror and back to her anxious face. "Lea, are you going to plan every inch of this journey ahead of time? Calculate odds and probabilities and error margins of every conceivable action?"

"If I can."

He took a step back and raised his hands, feeling more and more grumpy by the minute. "Fine. Plan away. Just leave me out of it. This is just getting too absurd."

Her eyes narrowed, in anger now. "Leave you out of it? That kind of defeats the entire point of you being here, isn't it? You're the expert. You're here to help me out, aren't you? This is a big step. I don't want to mess it up."

"Well, think about what you're asking here! I'm not giving you blueprint of a first kiss, Lea. Forget it."

"Can't you give me some hints?"

Thomas felt like punching the nearest wall. With his head. "What the hell do you want from me, Lea? A demonstration?"

"Of course not," she growled at him, but then her growl became a whisper. "You think I'm being ridiculous, don't you?"

"Well, yes. Since you ask, you *are* being rather ridiculous."

"You think I'm being stupid and pathetic, don't you?"

"No!" How he longed to grab her and shake sense into her sometimes. "Lea, stop being so bloody insecure. It's annoying!"

"*Annoying?* I'm *annoying* you?"

"Yes! It drives me nuts to see you do that. You're a lovely, smart, funny, attractive woman. You've got nothing to be insecure about."

"You think—"

He'd never subscribed to the theory that shutting women up with a kiss was ever a particularly wise thing to do, but suddenly he found himself doing just that *again.* Her lips were warm and inviting, even when frozen in surprise, and she responded after just a fraction of a second. He relaxed when he felt her arms go around his neck and allowed himself to forget every reason why they shouldn't be kissing.

It worked. The world vanished into nothing but Tom-and-Lea and the taste and scent of her drowned his last remaining brain cells.

The doorbell interrupted, and they jumped apart. As far as they could, with his fingers tangled in her hair. He swore, and disentangled himself without looking at her face.

"There," he said gruffly and turned away to stare out the window, just as she blinked, and looked at him with wide astonished eyes, asking questions he didn't know the answers to. He rested his forehead on the cold windowpane, vaguely surprised that it didn't sizzle at the contact. "You got your blueprint for a first kiss. Happy now?"

Where had that explanation come from? He didn't want Lea kissing Paul like that. He didn't want her kissing anyone like that. But that was the only logical explanation, wasn't it? The only explanation he was prepared to give for what had just happened.

"See," he added. "A kiss is no big deal, is it? Nothing to worry about."

"Right," she said. Her voice sounded steady to him, not at all raw like his. "A kiss is no big deal. Got it. Thanks for the demonstration, Thomas."

Sarcasm? He glanced over his shoulder at her face, but she had turned away from him and was walking toward the front door just as the doorbell chimed again.

Thomas clenched his fists until he felt his nails bore into his palms. What now? She'd go out there and kiss that guy because he'd told her it was *no big deal?* "Don't do anything you don't want to, Lea." His voice was gruff, and he cleared his throat and turned away to stare out the window again. "You said it didn't feel right, so don't do it. The game is adjustable, you know. You can bend the rules. You can break them. You can even make up your own as you go along."

He didn't know if she'd heard. Her words drifted to him, low and calm. Not at all like the state of his own mind. Hadn't she been affected at all? "Goodbye, Thomas. You just let yourself out whenever." Then he heard the front door open, and her greet Paul.

He folded his arms, and pressed his forehead harder into the window, pretending he wasn't straining to hear every word.

Then the door closed and they were gone.

Thomas fell into her sofa and lay down, his gaze exploring every inch of the ceiling before his eyes closed tightly. Lea was on her own. Could she handle it?

Could *he* handle it?

She should have asked him to come along.

He leapt to his feet, grabbed his leather jacket from where he'd flung it over a recliner, and raced out the door.

*   *   *

Paul didn't seem to notice anything was amiss, but it was hard to keep her attention on him, and not on that fierce kiss she'd just shared with Thomas. Again. There was a pattern here. She referred to herself as stupid, and he kissed her to shut her up.

Why?

And why did she have to like it far too much? Why had she wanted to ignore the doorbell, and the perfectly nice man waiting for her, and instead fall on the sofa with Thomas for a prolonged lesson in taking-things-to-the-next-level?

She wanted to cry, Lea decided. Yes. That was what she wanted to do. Curl up with Uruk and give her a salty bath. Cat's purr was a great antidote to a broken heart.

Broken heart?

She stabbed a tomato with her fork, and stared at the juice that oozed out. She hadn't done anything so stupid as to fall for Thomas, had she? Her heart started racing as she analyzed her feelings for Thomas and her feelings for Paul—and the depth of difference between what she felt for each man.

Damn it all.

She took a deep breath, forcing herself to shut the lid on those thoughts. She was looking for a husband, a father for her children, not someone who'd join the French Foreign Legion at the merest risk of commitment.

She looked up at her date and smiled at him, apologizing for having drifted out of touch for a moment. Paul smiled back, and she concentrated on their conversation, reminding herself to count her blessings. She had a handsome, nice man here, with a charming personality, someone who wanted the same things in life as she did.

It was just the kisses, she decided. She'd kissed Thomas—not Paul—and he'd been the first man she'd kissed in a whole year. Of course she'd been affected. It was all physical. Could have been any man.

Could have been Paul if she'd kissed him first.

Tonight, it *would* be Paul.

Already as he arrived at the restaurant, he could see through the window that Lea's date with Paul seemed—as usual—to be going great. Damn it. They were talking and laughing. She wasn't suffering any nerves. Of course, if she'd already made up her mind to kiss the guy, having made that decision would take the edge off the anxiety.

He ground his teeth at the thought, and bullied the waiter until he could get a table within eyeshot of the couple. Unfortunately, the only available table put him in a spot where Paul could see him, but Lea could not.

On second thought, that might be a good thing, he decided as he randomly picked something off the menu. Paul didn't know him, and Lea might not appreciate him following her without permission.

What are you doing? a sane voice inside his head finally asked, about the time his lobster soup arrived. He put down his spoon, and listened. *You're jealous, Tom,* the voice continued relentlessly. *And what are you going to do about it? Are you going to father her baby for her?* He found himself shaking his head. *Of course you're not. So, that leaves us with the original question: What are you doing?*

Thomas groaned, and narrowed his eyes to send a particularly evil glare Lea's way. He didn't have an answer, and in those situations there was only one thing to do with annoying internal voices.

Ignore them.

Stalker.

He'd turned into a stalker, following them as Paul drove Lea home after an eternity spent at the restaurant, and another eternity at a nearby bar, where they'd *danced,* for God's sake. Of course, he was just looking after Lea's best interests, doing what she'd asked him to do on three occasions before. Only difference was, this time she didn't know she had a bodyguard watching out for her.

He parked two houses away and walked the rest, timing it so that he was close to the front yard as Lea was saying goodbye—or that was what he hoped she was saying—at her front door. Feeling more and more like a stalker, he paused in the shadow of a tree and watched them chat and laugh for a while. Then Lea paused and started rummaging in her purse for her key.

Thomas felt his whole body tense and a cloud of doom descended upon him. She wasn't going to ask Paul in, was she? No. No way. It was way too soon for that. They hadn't even kissed yet. He couldn't let her do that.

Paul raised his hand and touched Lea's shoulder, and before Thomas knew what he was doing he was striding up the front path, and the couple had sprung apart. Both were staring at him, one in surprise, one in insulted fury.

He'd deal with that later. He knew he was doing the right thing.

"Lea!" He smiled so widely he thought he heard his jaw crack and grabbed her for a bear hug, lifting her up and swinging her around for good measure. "Hi, honey. I decided to drop by and chat."

"Weren't you at the restaurant?" Paul asked, his thumb pointing back over his shoulder, toward the city center. "I'm sure I saw you. Single table by the kitchen door?"

Thomas grinned. "You're observant."

"You were at the restaurant?" Lea asked. Thomas smiled at her. He held his arm firmly over Lea's shoulder despite her attempt to shrug it off. "You're Paul. I'm Thomas. Close friend of Lea's. Maybe she's mentioned me?"

"No, I don't think so. Well..." He looked at Lea. "Everything okay?"

Lea nodded. She seemed incapable of speaking, but Thomas suspected that would only last as long as it took for her to get her temper into gear. He was in for some serious lashing.

Paul looked between him and Lea, looking indecisive. "Well, I should be going. You're sure everything's okay?"

Lea stammered something. Then she nodded. He could feel her body trembling, and as Paul left and her gaze rose slowly, revealing eyes so dark he could no longer see any green, he was pretty sure what emotion caused that.

Anger.

And all directed at him.

Reality returned, smirking at him.

What had he done? Why?

Lea slammed the key in the lock and opened the door. He shouldered his way inside, as she would have shut the door in his face. He slammed the door behind them, feeling his own anger build.

"What was that all about?" she spat at him.

Thomas leaned against the wall and scowled back at her while he tried to remember what that *had* been all about. "You were going to invite him inside, weren't you?" he accused. "A few hours ago you hated the idea of kissing him, and now here you were, inviting him in!"

"So? He was telling me a long story about something at work, so I invited him in for a minute, rather than sit forever in the car."

"You don't really think he was coming in to *chat*, do you?"

"Why not? Not all men interpret an invitation for coffee as an invitation to bed, Thomas."

"Most do," he grunted. She couldn't be that naive, trusting a complete stranger she'd only met a handful of times.

"And what if I did invite him to stay the night? Why shouldn't I? Oh, of course," she taunted. "You're afraid I'd get it wrong, drive him off and ruin all your hard work. You'd have to do everything all over again."

He kept scowling. "Not exactly."

"Then what?" She stared at him for a while, waiting for a response, but he didn't have one. Anger was making her cheeks red, and her eyes flash with emerald fire. "God, Thomas, do you realize what you behaved like out there? What you looked like? You might as well have threatened him with a club. Now he thinks you're my ex stalking me or something. You're probably lucky he didn't call the police and report imminent domestic violence." She stomped around, fuming, and tore off her coat and heels. "I bet he won't even call me again, and it'll be your fault."

"Well, good riddance."

She put her hands on her hips and stared at him. "He could be the one, you know. Everything's been going perfectly."

"Perfectly?" he howled. "A couple of hours ago you were practically throwing up at the idea of kissing that guy!"

She shrugged. "Just nerves. He likes me. I like him. It would have gone fine if you'd have let me kiss him!"

Would have. So they hadn't kissed in the car. He smiled with satisfaction. Bad move. Lea shook her head in disgust, took a step closer until she was standing only two feet away and raised her voice in one last astonished shout at him. "What exactly is your problem, Thomas?"

She looked wonderful. Her eyes ablaze with emotion and her whole being concentrated on him—which was a good thing. He was tempted. He was very tempted to grab her, growl "This is my problem," and kiss her until she forgot all about probability theory. But he didn't. Instead he turned around and stalked toward the kitchen. "I need a drink," he threw over his shoulder.

"Do help yourself," she said, not sounding very hospitable at all as she followed him through the house. "You know well enough where I keep it, and you're too big for me to throw out of the house. Why were you at the restaurant in the first place?"

"Good thing I was, wasn't it? You obviously still don't know what you're doing."

She was standing in the kitchen door, leaning against the doorjamb with her arms crossed when he'd located a beer at the back of her fridge, anger and confusion flashing from her eyes, along with a dab of misery he didn't like seeing there.

"I don't understand you, Thomas. We've been working at this together for weeks. Why would you try to ruin everything?"

He popped the beer open and took a swig. He didn't close the fridge immediately . He could use some cool air right now. "Simple. That guy's not right for you. You need more."

"I don't need more. I just need someone—"

"Suitable," he interrupted. "I know. You're told me often enough what you're looking for. Well, forget it. He's not it."

"Why? Did you find out something new about him?"

"Yeah."

Her stance changed, and her voice lost some of its fury. "You did? What was it? Something bad?"

He took a long drink of the beer, trying to regain control over his tongue. What was he saying? "Yeah. Something bad," he heard himself mutter.

Worry faded out the remaining anger in her eyes and she leaned against a wall, hugging herself. She looked alone and miserable. At the thought of losing *Paul,* for God's sake. The thought ripped at his gut and jealousy twisted his stomach. "Oh, my God," she whispered. "Of course there had to be something wrong. Tell me, Thomas. What is it? He's married, isn't he?"

He shook his head. He'd been walking on thin ice all evening, but it had finally cracked. There was no way back now.

"Something even worse?"

He shrugged.

"Oh, God, Thomas, don't tell me he's a criminal?"

"No."

Impatience and fear knotted her brow. She walked

closer until only two feet separated them and put her hand on his chest, pushing her fist into his skin in her impatience to get the words out of him. Her touch burned, but he didn't flinch from it. It felt too damned good. "Well, what is it, then, Thomas? What's wrong with him? Tell me!"

He rubbed his face with his hands a few times before answering, but sanity didn't return despite the desperate delaying tactics. The words were already on the tip of his tongue, fighting to get out, and there was nothing he could to do stop them. Taking one deep breath of invigorating air, cool from the still open fridge, he looked up, fixed her with his gaze and said it.

"He's not me."

CHAPTER EIGHT

HIS words hovered in the air between them for a long time. Thomas felt dizzy, waiting for her response. He wasn't sure what he was hoping for, but he found himself holding his breath.

She swallowed. Then she pulled her hand away from his chest and took a step back. She hugged herself, her arms tight around her middle. Her anger had evaporated, leaving confusion and misery in her eyes. "What are you saying, Thomas?" she whispered. "What do you mean, he's not you?"

He slammed his beer down, kicked the fridge door shut with his knee, and took a step forward. That left only a few inches between them again, and he could smell her scent, hear her breath. He trembled with the effort of not touching her. She didn't back further off, but her dark eyes held shock as she looked up at him.

"When I think about you kissing him, I feel like my insides are being torn apart," he whispered harshly. "When I see him hold your hand, I want to rip his arms off. When I see you laugh with him, I want to put him on the first flight to Singapore and then shut down international air trafficking."

"Thomas…"

"I want you," he said starkly. "I want you for myself."

Silence deafened the air for a long while. As she exhaled her breath brushed his chin. "Thomas…" Her voice was barely a whisper. The darkness in her eyes told him his admission meant something to her. He raised a hand to her face and tucked a strand of hair behind her ear. His hand lingered, tracing the curve of her ear, down to her neck, then to her nape. The inches between them seemed to evaporate without either of them moving.

She felt so good in his arms. Her cheek was soft against his, her hair equally soft under his hand. He kissed her skin, her scent gentle and distracting. He felt her lips move against his cheek, not in a caress, but struggling to form words. He heard nothing, except the catch of her breath. What was she trying to say? Tell him to stop, tell him to go on? Telling him to get the hell out of her life, or to stop the damn dithering and kiss her properly?

She didn't have all the time in the world. If she wanted to escape, she could, but she only had a few more moments until he'd claim her.

Mine. She's *mine.* The possessive feeling was ridiculous, but only made him tighten his arms around her even more, desperate to keep her as close as possible. She could have a couple more seconds to tell him to get the hell away from her, but that was it.

Or was it? She wasn't his. He shouldn't want her, not when she came with such a complete package of expectations, but he did. She shouldn't want him—but she was telling him now, without any words, that she did.

Still…

Why didn't he kiss her already? Lea thought—as much as she could think anything under the circumstances, enveloped in his arms, with his lips touching her cheek so gently, his fingers tangled in her hair. Thomas wanted her. If his words hadn't been convincing enough, she had the truth in the tension of his body, the way his heart pounded against her in a frantic race with her own heart.

Her hands were trapped between them. She pushed to get them free, and to her panic Thomas began to release her. She pressed herself against him, and felt him take a step back until his back was to the fridge. She followed, lifting her head to look into his eyes for one second before wrapping her arms around him, her fingers trailing up his neck into his hair, pushing at the back of his head until he was once again close enough to kiss.

But he was resisting, his gaze searching her face as if trying to decipher the true meaning of life.

"Thomas?" she murmured. "I'm trying to kiss you. Cooperate, please."

His mouth twisted in a small smile, but there was panic in his eyes along with the hesitation. She recognized it easily, and her heart sank. Of course he was afraid. He'd think she wanted more than he wanted to give. He'd probably be ordering the ticket to Pakistan tomorrow morning. She smiled, suddenly feeling protective of him. "It's okay, Thomas," she whispered. "I know. You're not what I'm looking for, and I'm not what you're looking for. It's okay. We can still have…one little kiss, can't we? What harm can that do?"

The panic in his eyes clouded into confusion and indecision. He started to speak, and she used the opportunity and breached his last defenses, wrapping her arms tighter around his neck and pressing her mouth to his. She nibbled on his lips until his resistance crumbled and smiled against his mouth when he turned hungry, then greedy, cradling her face in his hands as he kissed her as if he could never get enough.

He'd never get enough of her.

"Oh, God, Lea," he muttered, burying his face in her neck. He was trembling. Or maybe she was. It was hard to tell, and he wouldn't rule out an earthquake either. "Maybe we should..." He wasn't sure what he was going to say? Stop?

No. No way.

Get rid of all these annoying clothes?

Yes. Absolutely.

His fingers already started edging toward the hem of her sweater before he clenched his hand into a fist.

No. Not yet. They needed to talk.

No, they didn't need to talk. The last thing they needed to do right now was to talk. "Lea, are you sure this is...I mean, do you..."

He felt her take a breath and open her mouth to interrupt his ramblings, and braced himself. She grabbed the front of his shirt and buried her face in his neck. "Shut up, Thomas," she growled in his ear, her mouth opening on his neck.

Thank God.

Then they were kissing again, and he didn't care any more if they needed to talk or not.

Until the phone rang, on the kitchen wall a few feet away, startling them enough to jump apart. Lea stared at him, breathing hard, then snatched the phone off the wall and all but barked into it.

It was Paul, obviously, checking if she was okay, safe from the madman who'd accosted them at the door. Good of him, Thomas grudgingly admitted, even as jealousy began slicing up his gut again. Lea assured

Paul she was okay, thanked him and hung up. Her back was to him, shoulders slumped, but he could see her straighten up before she slowly turned around to face him.

Her clothes were a mess wherever his hands had seen an opportunity to sneak under and touch bare skin, and her hair—well, nothing that an hour with a hairdresser wouldn't fix, he supposed. It had been worth it, even if he had to fix the damage himself.

Yes. He could do that. He could wash her hair, dry it, carefully work out the tangles until everything was once again silky and warm, ready to be ravished along with the rest of her.

''Oh my God,'' she whispered, shattering his newly discovered hairdresser fantasy. ''What were we doing?''

Disoriented, he shook his head. It didn't take a genius to figure out she was withdrawing from him. The shock in her eyes was close to horror. He crossed his arms on his chest and shrugged. ''Do you really want me to answer that?''

''No.''

''Good. Because if you don't know what we were doing, you need more detailed lessons than I've been giving you.''

She crossed her arms, unconsciously mimicking his own pose. ''I see. This was all a part of the dating curriculum?''

Thomas closed his eyes. She was too tempting to look at. ''I'm not dignifying that with an answer.'' Then he did. ''You know it wasn't.''

''Why did you do it?''

''Do what? You kissed me, remember?''

''Yes, but only after you told me…''

"That I wanted you. Yes. I do." He opened his eyes. "I do. I want you. I want this, and much more. It's pretty obvious what I want, isn't it?"

For a long moment their gazes clung together, until she shook her head and looked away. "Yes. A fling," she said slowly. "That's what you want, isn't it? Like you said—a carefree relationship with someone you're attracted to. No strings, no future involving children or a family. That's what you want with me, isn't it? That what you think I should want, before settling down with someone. You want us to have a fling."

He supposed. What else could he want? His nod was only halfhearted though. He wanted *her*. That was the key word.

"It won't work, Thomas. I'm not the type to have flings. I don't do that sort of thing. You know what I want," she said, her voice trembling. "And even though I—" She stopped what she was saying and shook her head. "You're…not what I want," she added in a hoarse whisper that tore at his soul. "You're not stable, responsible, suitable—you told me so yourself. You're not what I want, Thomas, you're not."

"And he is?" he bellowed, arm slashing through the air to point toward the front door as pain squeezed his heart. "That guy's what you want?"

Her nod was minuscule, but it told him everything. "He is. He's right for me. You're…not."

He swallowed. "Maybe I'm not what you think I am," he said, his voice forced. Her eyes were very green as she stared back at him and they were brimmed with longing that filled him with hope and despair both at once.

"Aren't you?"

Her soft question echoed in the kitchen, inviting an answer he didn't know how to give.

He wasn't what she wanted.

That was a wall he could not climb over. And she was right. Once before he'd become involved with a woman who wanted different things than he did—and rather than be trapped, he'd ended up fleeing as far as he could get. It wouldn't be any different this time. Why would it, when Lea had been so clear from the start about what her intentions were? It wasn't fair of him to play with her emotions like this. She'd told him in the very beginning what she wanted.

And why the hell wasn't he getting an uncontrollable urge to flee to Finland just thinking about the implications of what she wanted—if she wanted it from him?

"You made it clear, Thomas. You're not what I want…" Lea whispered again, and it hardened his heart in a reflex action of defense. How had he let her get to him like this, knowing neither of them was what the other wanted?

He shook his head, and somehow managed to send her a tight grin. "I know. I heard you the first time." He turned around to leave. "Goodbye, Lea."

"Thomas…"

There were tears in her voice. They chased him all the way home.

"You're far away tonight."

Lea dragged her gaze away from the sculpture she'd been staring at for several minutes and tried to smile at Paul.

"I'm sorry," she said. "I have some things on my mind. I didn't mean to be boring company."

"You're not," Paul objected. He took her hand, pulling her along to the next sculpture. No sparks shot up her hand. No tingles went up her spine. Phooey.

This wasn't fair. Paul was right for her. Why did she keep wishing he made her feel like Thomas did, when Thomas was so utterly wrong for her?

"This one's interesting," Paul commented.

Lea stared at the sculpture. A huge boulder of rock, vaguely resembling a planet in shape, melted in places to create the illusion of continents, with small pieces of colorful plastic toys sticking out of the melted surface. It was called *Child's Play.*

It was perfect. A perfect example of what Thomas would call a horrible piece of art. He'd say *art* in that unique way he had, painting quotes around the words with his voice.

He was *such* a philistine.

"Judging by the size of that smile, you must really like this one," Paul said.

Lea nodded and felt the smile fade away from her lips. "Yeah. I love it. It's a truly horrible piece of art, isn't it?" she said wistfully, not really knowing what she was saying until Paul gave her a quizzical look.

Stop it, Lea! she tried to tell herself. Thomas wasn't what she wanted. She wasn't what he wanted either—except in one specific way that she could have sworn wasn't what she wanted right now.

So why couldn't she put him out of her mind?

She wanted a family, a baby—she wouldn't ruin that plan by chasing rainbows again.

But there was no denying it—as evidenced by how *Child's Play* reminded her of him—she missed Thomas. She missed him, as the friend he'd become.

And, she admitted to herself with a sigh, she also

missed him as the lover that despite everything she wanted him to become.

He wasn't what she wanted, and she'd told him that.

It had been the truth in one way—but a lie in another sense. He had to have known that, of course. But she had a specific goal, a specific agenda—and he was nothing but an obstacle to her plans.

She was no longer standing in front of the sculpture. Paul had maneuvered them through the gallery and to the small coffee shop near the entrance, and she hadn't even noticed until he'd already ordered for them and found seats.

"We just got here," she said, but gratefully grasped her cup of coffee. "Don't you want to see the rest of the exhibit?"

"Yeah. But it isn't much fun with a comatose woman at my side."

Just her luck, ending up with a perceptive guy. "Sorry. I do that sometimes when I've got something on my mind."

"We need to talk, don't we?"

"That sounds ominous," Lea said. What now?

Was she about to get dumped?

"That guy at your house the other day…"

"Yes? What about him?" Her voice was defensive, and she tried to soften it with a smile. "Bit of a dragon, wasn't he? He's pretty protective of me."

Paul's eyes crinkled at the corners when he grinned. He was such a nice man, Lea thought wistfully. If only there were any sparks between them. "Yeah. A male dragon fighting for his lady. Right?"

Something stuck in her throat. She couldn't speak, but that seemed enough of an answer for Paul.

"I'm not sure why you're seeing me," he continued,

"when there's obviously something serious between you two."

"It's complicated," Lea mumbled. "Nothing's really between us. Thomas is…well, we don't want the same things in life. His feelings for me aren't…" She groaned. "Well, let's just say it's complicated."

Paul shrugged. "From what I saw you have *something,* which is an excellent beginning." He stirred his coffee, still holding her gaze. "It's one we don't have, isn't it? We're compatible in many ways, but there's something lacking. Right?"

I *am* getting dumped, Lea thought with a sigh, even as she smiled and nodded at Paul with a certain amount of relief.

Back to the drawing board.

Danny was one day away from having his first birthday.

Which meant Lea was two days away from having her thirtieth birthday.

It was looking even bleaker now. Not only had she lost the prospective husband, she'd also lost her mentor. She'd also lost a little thing called a heart, but she was working hard at repressing that fact, stomping it deep into the dark dirty layers where she kept regrets and painful memories.

But in the greater scheme of things—like putting together an authentic snake cake—tiny things like broken hearts were pretty insignificant, weren't they?

"I don't think snakes have blue eyes," Lea grumbled as she tried to stick blue candies to the snake's head. "I can't believe we're actually going to paint a tri-colored pattern on this thing."

"Danny's already showing interest in nature," Anne

said, busy with the snake's tail end, which was supposed to rattle as the cake was cut. As if anyone would be able to hear *anything* with eight toddlers at the table tomorrow. "I want this to be a genuine rattlesnake with a pattern as close as we can get to the real thing."

"Venom and all?"

"Very funny. No, it's a nonvenomous snake. How's your boyfriend from the dating agency?"

"Oh, pretty much nonvenomous."

"What's going on? Have you needed that bedroom checklist yet?"

Lea stirred the green frosting and started applying the first color. "None of your business."

"You never tell me anything anymore," Anne complained. "You're still seeing him, aren't you? You haven't moved on to a new guy?"

"No new guy."

"And how's Thomas? Still helping out?"

"No. He got me through the early stages. Now I'm on my own."

"I see."

"Hand me the yellow frosting, please."

"There's something you aren't telling me, isn't there?"

"There's a lot I'm not telling you." Things were far too confusing at the moment to tell Anne anything. She wouldn't even know where to start.

Anne sighed. "You're not going to tell me, are you? Fine. Only one thing to do, then."

"What?"

"Get you drunk. That'll get you talking. What are you doing for your birthday?"

"Now that you mention it, getting drunk probably isn't the worst idea."

"We're partying, right?"

"Mmm," Lea said noncommittally. "I don't know. I don't have any plans. I'm probably in denial. Maybe I'll just light a candle for my lost youth and spend an evening meditating on what to do with my golden years."

"Come on! You have to do something to celebrate." She snapped her fingers. "I know—your birthday is the day after Danny's. We'll have the party here. We can use some of the same stuff and we won't have to move the furniture again. The place will even be toddler-safe, which means it's also drunk-adults safe."

"Oh boy. Milk and leftover rattlesnake cake for my thirtieth birthday. I can't wait."

Anne's stern look would have been more impressive without the green and yellow frosting smeared on her cheek. "I'm throwing you a party. That's final."

By the time Lea was getting a wet goodbye kiss from the birthday boy, she'd given in to Anne's offer.

It wasn't as if she had anything better planned for her birthday.

Besides, she rationalized as she started her car and started heading back home, getting drunk and blathering about Thomas to her friends was probably a lot healthier than curling up in bed with a basketful of chocolate and blathering about Thomas to her cat.

CHAPTER NINE

LEA shuffled along the toy store aisle, feeling indescribably morose.

This was her last day of being twenty-nine. Tomorrow she was thirty.

Thirty.

It boggled the mind. How had this happened to her? *When* had this happened?

Thirty was mature, grown-up age. Know-what-to-do-with-my-life age. Wife-and-Mom age.

And she didn't even have someone special to wake up with tomorrow morning, someone who'd put his arms around her with a sleepy smile, whispering that he still loved her even though she'd turned into an old lady overnight.

There was a giant stuffed panther guarding the entrance to the stuffed animals aisle. It had blue eyes. It sent her pulse racing in a way no stuffed animal ever had before.

Damn Thomas.

Lea cursed and turned in the other direction. Anne had suggested "something educational" for her son, anyway.

She yanked a Science-Experiments-for-Toddlers kit out of a shelf and turned into the noisy aisle in search of something that would make Danny laugh, even if it didn't make any promises to raise his IQ.

She didn't have anything to complain about, she reminded herself. She *did* know what to do with her life.

She was happy with the education she'd chosen, she had a good job that she loved. There wasn't any real identity crisis on the horizon in that respect. She knew what she wanted to do with the professional part of her life.

She stopped in front of the musical instruments display and frowned, fists clenched in indecisive frustration. Okay, no problems on the professional front.

It was just the personal part that needed serious adjustment. Some serious punching and kicking and beating into submission.

"A drum set?"

"It's therapeutic for him," Lea said in her own defense. "When he's upset or angry, he can bang and hit all he wants, get it all out of his system. And develop his artistic and motor skills all at the same time."

Anne summoned her husband and pointed at the evidence. "Brian, Lea bought our one-year-old son a drum set."

Brian looked at the box and his expression of horror matched his wife's. "I told you sooner or later she would punish us for fixing her up with James."

"Oh, stop complaining. I got him a science kit too. Look—he's already discovered that his head fits inside the box if you throw all the boring educational stuff out of it."

Anne picked up her birthday boy and snatched the box off his head. "Do parental earmuffs come with the drum set?"

"Afraid not."

Anne sent her a mock glare. "Fine. New house rule: Danny can play his drums every time Aunt Lea is visiting."

The doorbell chimed and Danny was dumped in Lea's arms. "Help the birthday boy answer the door, will you? I'll see about the coffee. Sounds like people are early."

Lea carried the child to the door, and opened it, in no way prepared for who was behind it.

"Thomas?" she asked, almost stuttering in disbelief.

He still had the bluest eyes ever. The panther had nothing on him.

He shrugged. "Yeah. It's me."

"What are you doing here?" God, it was good to see him again. She'd never quite understood the meaning of the phrase "sight for sore eyes", but she did now.

She wasn't quite sure she could believe her eyes, though, but Danny was squirming and giggling and seemed to recognize the intruder. It might have had something to do with the huge parcel Thomas was carrying. The kid caught on quick.

"Tom!" Anne swept past her and hugged Thomas, then grabbed Danny from her arms and dumped him on Thomas.

What the hell was going on here?

There was only one way to get the answer to that question. She stepped forward and cleared her throat. "What's going on? I didn't know you two knew each other."

Thomas looked guilty. Anne just looked pleased. "Surprise! Your Thomas is my stepbrother Tom. You know, the new stepbrother I acquired a couple of years ago?"

Whoa.

She looked at Thomas. "You knew...?" She'd mentioned again and again that she felt safe with Thomas because he was a stranger, because what was between them was confidential, not something that her friends would be discussing between them. Sure, Anne knew what was going on, but she'd been the only one. Thomas didn't look surprised to see her. He must have known all along…

"It was my fault," Anne interrupted. "I was the one who asked him to look out for you."

"Look out for me?"

"On your…date…with James…" Anne looked between the two and seemed to realize she should have better left that unsaid. "I mean…"

Things were starting to make horrible sense. "You mean—it was all a setup? You sent Thomas to spy on me on my date?" Her voice rose in pitch. "You got Thomas to rescue me from James?"

"It wasn't like that, Lea," Anne said. "I was worried about you. I just wanted someone to be there in case things got ugly."

"It was my idea to rescue you," Thomas added gruffly. "It wasn't part of the plan. It was just…crazy impulsiveness. And then I couldn't tell you since Anne swore me to secrecy." He met her eyes briefly and shrugged. "I'm sorry. I didn't mean to deceive you."

"I was afraid you wouldn't want Thomas's help any more if you knew I knew him," Anne said. "And you were so pleased with your plan. So I used emotional blackmail to get him to keep his mouth shut."

Lea held her breath for a long moment until she could be sure her voice wouldn't just be a series of random squeaks. Then she waved a hand at them, dismissing the two worried faces. "Don't worry. It's fine. I understand."

The anxiety in the two faces was replaced with confusion.

"You're not mad?" Anne asked.

"No."

"You're not going to tell us you can handle your own life and we just better not get in your way?"

"No. Thank you Anne, for wanting to look after me. And thank you Thomas, for…helping out. I appreciate it. Now, I believe I have a rattlesnake to transport to the dining room."

Anne caught up with her in the kitchen, just as she was balancing the large plate with the rattlesnake cake in her arms, trying not to think about anything at all. First she needed to make sure her emotions were under control—then she could allow her thoughts to muddle up the picture. "Lea, what's wrong?"

"I don't know what happened to the frosting overnight, but this is now purple, not green."

"I don't care," Anne said impatiently. "I couldn't care less what color the damn snake is. Why aren't you furious?"

"Why should I be? You had my best interests at heart. So did Thomas. Nothing to be upset about."

"We deceived you. We practically lied to you. I tried to control your life. You should be mad."

"I'm not mad." She managed to keep her voice perfectly level and took vicious pleasure in seeing how much that annoyed Anne. "Does the candle go on the cake now?"

"Lea!"

Lea met her friend's frustrated gaze without flinching and raised an eyebrow. "It's your son's first birthday, Anne. Get the candle."

*   *   *

Lea's heart was pounding as she sat across from Thomas and tried to eat a piece of the purple rattlesnake. He was avoiding her eyes and pushing his cake listlessly around on the cartoon plate, but for the moment that didn't matter, just looking at him felt good.

She'd been angry for a minute, yes, hearing how he and Anne had been sneaking around behind her back, but both of them had meant well. In hindsight, she now understood the pained look on Thomas's face when she'd repeatedly told him she wanted his help because he was a stranger. She hadn't really given him a chance to exit the situation without making her feel hurt and humiliated, at being either turned down or told the truth. He'd only been trying to spare her feelings.

But what had really paralyzed all the anger out of her was that without their interference, she might never have gotten to know Thomas at all. They'd have met, right here at this party today, maybe shaken hands and talked about Danny's new toys, and then they'd have walked out of each other's life without ever experiencing all that had happened between them now. She couldn't bear even thinking about it.

It had all been worth it.

That single realization had knocked away the last barriers from her heart. She'd realized the minute she'd seen Thomas again that it wasn't just because he wasn't husband-and-father material that she'd pushed him away. That wasn't even the main reason.

It was because she was afraid of the intensity of her feelings for him, afraid of again being left hurt and alone. That was a fear she'd never felt, contemplating a relationship with Paul, because losing him would never have mattered this much.

All through the party, she waited for an opportunity

to get Thomas alone, to talk to him—to tell him…No, she didn't know what she wanted to tell him, but she might figure it out, if she could just get him somewhere private. There was a look in his eyes that convinced her that she wanted to…take a chance.

But the chaos that came with all the toddlers and their parents, along with Danny's grandparents and assorted other relatives and friends, wasn't conducive to private conversations. By the time things quieted down a bit and she began looking around to see if Thomas was available to be dragged away for a talk, he was nowhere to be found.

"Where's Thomas?" she asked Brian as he passed her, carrying Danny on one arm and the drum set in the other. It had been a popular entertainment item today.

"I think he left a while ago."

Damn it.

She'd lost her chance to talk to him face to face.

Although she could always call him.

Or…

Yes.

So—what did an almost-thirty-year-old woman wear on her way to start her very first *fling?*

As soon as Lea got home she headed straight for her bedroom, threw the closet doors open and examined the contents with a critical eye.

Something red. Thomas had said she looked good in red.

She grinned, feeling determined and light-headed as she glanced at her watch. The shops should still be open. Yes, she'd definitely wear red.

*   *   *

It was almost two hours later when she stopped her car outside Thomas's house. The tall apartment building looked gloomy in the pouring rain. Definitely umbrella time.

When she'd locked the car and started walking toward the house, insecurity made an appearance for the first time since she'd decided what she wanted to do on her last night before she tumbled into her thirties.

What would he say?

He certainly hadn't said much, back at the birthday party. She braced her umbrella against the rain pounding from the east, and stalled, walking a block down the street and back again before telling herself she was being ridiculous. She entered the lobby and pressed the button on the intercom.

Maybe he wouldn't even be at home. She wasn't sure whether to hope for that or not, but she didn't have much time to agonize. His voice reached into her heart, and she knew she'd made the right decision. She grinned widely as she answered him. "Hi, Thomas."

Pause. "Lea?"

"Yeah, it's me."

"Come on up."

The elevator was big. It had mirrors. She studiously avoided looking into them. There was no telling what kind of a message her own eyes would give her.

Then the elevator opened, and Thomas was standing there in an open doorway just across the hall.

She'd come to him.

Thomas stared at her approach, confused, but first and foremost thrilled. He'd planned to pay her an unannounced visit tomorrow, on her birthday. That was all he'd planned, not knowing if she wanted to see him

again. He hadn't dared approach her at Anne's house.
Too many possible pitfalls. Not to mention witnesses.
Her lack of reaction to the way he and Anne had been
deceiving her had been alarming.

But now she was here—unless he was dreaming,
which wasn't a farfetched conclusion.

"Hi, Thomas," she said, trying to smile. It was a
wobbly smile, but it warmed his heart. She was clutching an umbrella, still open above her head. He gestured
at it.

"Was it raining in the elevator?"

Lea glanced up at the umbrella. "Uh, no. I guess I
had other things on my mind." Smiling sheepishly, she
closed the umbrella and shoved it in the umbrella stand
his mother had given him last Christmas. It held thir-
teen umbrellas at the last count. "No wonder your
neighbors on the third floor looked at me funny. Can I
come in?"

She was already inside, but he was standing directly
in front of her, as if to block her entrance farther into
the apartment. He stepped aside.

"Of course."

"Thank you."

"Are you still seeing Paul?"

She tilted her head to the side and grinned at him.
"You put an effective stop to that, didn't you?"

"I'm sorry if I ruined something for you." *No,
you're not*, his conscience taunted and he told it to shut
up. He wanted Lea to be happy. If another man made
her happy, then so be it. He wasn't about to become
breeding stock, anyway.

"Don't worry about it," she said.

He couldn't stand it any longer. She kept looking at
him, unflinching, and he couldn't look back.

"What is it, Lea? Why are you here?"

"I thought…I started thinking…"

"Yes?"

"That maybe you were wrong for me…but still in a way, you're right…" She stopped. Closed her mouth. Swallowed. "You know?"

"No, I don't know, Lea."

"You see, I didn't want to kiss Paul, remember? Not at all. But since you kissed me that first time, it's been on constant replay in my head. And you said you…" She took a deep breath. "You said you wanted me for yourself. Do you? Because, you see, I want you too. And maybe…a fling is a wonderful idea after all. Isn't it?"

He couldn't figure out a way to give her an answer that made sense, but he reached out anyway, and saw the doubt vanish from her eyes as he nodded in response to her question. He couldn't help himself, and his hands touched her shoulders softly because they were shaking in an effort not to yank her into his arms.

"Thomas?" Her voice was trembling. So was her entire body as he enveloped her in a tight, platonic bear hug. He squeezed as tight as he dared, and held her for the longest time, absorbing the feel and scent of her with his eyes shut tight.

After a while, she tried to get loose, but he didn't let her. "Thomas…?" she repeated, her hand touching the back of his head gingerly, then sliding into his hair, naturally, as if in preparation for his kiss. He opened his mouth and tasted her neck. She started trembling again and when he pulled back to look into her eyes, he shut the door on all the whys.

"Lea—" he started. But then her hand tightened in

his hair, and she smiled as she pulled his head down, and it was too late.

"Yes. You'll be my fling," she murmured.

Thomas found it hard to think clearly with her lips against his, but her peculiar emphasis on the word "fling" set off a bunch of alarm bells. "What do you mean?"

"You told me I should have one last fling, remember? Your expert opinion. I'm following it."

"I didn't mean…" Things were rapidly spinning out of control. What was she saying? She didn't want a fling. She wanted a husband. She wanted a father for her children. She didn't want him because she wanted someone stable. And now she wanted him—but just for one night? Was that what she meant?

And, damn it, what did *he* want? Would he ever figure that out?

"You're my fling, Thomas," she whispered. "I want you. And you want me to be your fling. That's why you broke up my date, remember? You told me you wanted this. Let's get it out of our system."

Her grin was *wicked.* He hadn't even known Lea could be wicked and it was a bit of a shock.

"Show me your bedroom," she commanded.

"What?"

"Not that I'm not open to other locations, but your bedroom would be a nice start, right? Where is it?"

He gestured, trying to gather his thoughts. They weren't cooperating, and had in fact fled the scene of the crime-to-be. Instead the arena was flooded with emotions and hormones. And before he knew it she'd dragged him in there, and onto the bed.

"But we—"

"No buts. Not tonight." Her hands found their way

under his shirt. "We've got better things to do to-night."

"No," he groaned. "I can't do this. We have to talk first…"

"Thomas Carlisle, if you leave this bed now, you better have a damned good excuse for it."

He risked her wrath and rolled out of the bed. He moved to the other side of the room, taking deep gulps of air in an effort to calm himself. "I do. I'm trying to be honorable, love."

Her hair was a mess. It looked wonderful. He wanted it under his hands. Flowing over his bare chest. Anywhere.

"Don't call me love unless you mean it," she ordered. "And right at this moment, I don't really need to know if you mean it. Just get back to bed. *Now!*"

He'd never before known himself to have a submissive streak, but that order was for some reason extremely sexy. "We need to talk."

"Tomorrow. Tomorrow we'll talk about why we're right and wrong for each other. Come here."

"No, don't take off your sweater—Lea!" He turned away and covered his eyes, although it was far, far too late. "Oh. God. Please put that back on."

"Okay," she replied after a moment. "You can look now."

He turned back. "You see, we—" He went silent, staring at her. He swallowed, quite unable to tear his gaze away. "You lied."

She smiled provocatively at him. "No. I just said you could look now. Are you going to come here and help me, or do I have to get all the rest off by myself?"

"Lea…"

"It's my birthday in a couple of hours, Thomas."

That convinced him.

Somehow, he was now standing by the bed, instead of flattened against the wall. He found himself sinking down to sit at the edge of the bed just as she threw her jeans across the room. He bent his head and kissed her knee, trailed his fingers down her leg to her instep. "I thought you were shy."

"Not with you."

"Why not?"

"Necessity," she murmured, shifting closer to him. "I'm not sure why, but I'm having to resort to drastic measures to seduce you."

"I think I like being seduced."

She smiled. "Good."

"Nice colors."

"Glad you think so. I put this on just for you."

"This was all planned?"

She lay back, looking supremely happy with herself. "I was hoping it would work, yep. And I remember you said red was my color."

"Lucky that you owned red…whatever this is."

"Well—I didn't. Not until today. I remembered you said red became me."

"You went out and bought red stuff because I said you looked good in red?"

She was turning a very pretty shade of red herself. All over, as far as he could see. "Well, I was following your expert opinion. I'd hired you for that purpose, remember?"

"I wasn't hired to give expert opinion on underwear."

"Who cares? Why are we still talking?"

"Excellent question." He closed her mouth with a kiss and kicked the doubt demons out of the room.

CHAPTER TEN

LEA opened her eyes and blinked, and wondered why she'd woken up smiling. Then she realized where she was, and why. With whom.

And when.

The day had dawned. The day she had dreaded for at least a year. Her thirtieth birthday.

And the first few minutes didn't look terrible. She wasn't gazing into a black hole of a future. Nope. She was gazing at a masculine chest, half an inch from her nose, and his bed was warmer than hers had ever been. If this was going to be a habit, she'd have to get an industrial strength alarm clock or she'd never be able to make it out of bed in the morning.

Maybe turning thirty wasn't so bad after all, she mused, snuggling even closer. Even the baby urge had faded somewhat over the past few weeks. It was still there, quietly ticking, but it had been superceded by another strong urge. A Thomas-urge.

And now she was feeling urgent again.

His shoulder was so warm under her hand that she couldn't help herself. She raised her head and butted her way into the curve of his neck. This bed was too big, she thought vaguely. Far too much potential to roll away from each other in the middle of the night. A single bed would do nicely as long as she was sharing it with this man. Maybe they could spend the next night in her bed, the tiny bed she'd bought the moment she became single. It was small enough to make sure they stayed entangled together the entire night.

"Morning," he said into her ear, a sleepy, sexy voice, and she smiled. It just happened, spreading all over her face until her cheeks hurt with happiness. She kissed his neck.

"Morning."

His arms tightened around her and she felt him kiss her hair. "Happy birthday, angel."

She propped herself up on her elbows and smiled down at him. "Thank you." She stretched, feeling wonderful. "And you were right about the fling. Just what I needed for my thirtieth birthday." Smiling, she kissed the corner of his mouth. "Thanks for being my fling."

A small frown was etched on his forehead. "Are we okay?"

She nodded. "I think so. Aren't we?"

"I'm okay. So…if you're okay, I guess that means we're okay."

"Okay," she said, deadpan, and the lines on his forehead cleared. Then she found herself on her back.

"You're teasing me, aren't you?"

"Yes."

"We're really okay? You're not going to want me to apologize to Paul?"

"Well, you probably do owe Paul an apology, Thomas…"

His hand covered her mouth. He moved, and flashes of memory from last night reminded her that there were in fact all sorts of advantages in having a big bed.

"Mumph," she mumbled into his palm. She reached out and grabbed his wrist. "What are you doing?"

"I don't have a birthday present to give you. I'm making up for it."

"Oh," she breathed. "When you put it like that..."

"I guess we should be getting up soon," Lea said lazily. "It's almost noon, isn't it? I need to get going."

Thomas nodded absently, but was nowhere near ready to let her leave.

He had a lot of thinking to do.

During their week apart, he'd done even more, and his decision had been made even before the miracle had happened and Lea had come to him. He would have gone to her, and used every trick he could think of to seduce her into giving them another chance.

He hadn't been looking to settle down—but if a husband was what Lea was looking for, then maybe he could be it. He was in love, damn it. Enough to abandon the principles he'd held on to for so long. And what were the reasons for those principles? They'd seemed so important once, but now he couldn't remember.

He could even picture a couple of children in his near future. He wasn't sure he was quite ready to become a father right away, but that part might be negotiable. Maybe she'd agree to wait just a couple of years while he got used to the idea. Compromise was a part of every relationship.

At any rate, he'd always have nine months of her all to himself.

"Penny for them?"

He grinned at her. "I don't think you want to know."

"Something bad?"

"No." He traced the bridge of her nose with his

thumb. ''Just something I need to get organized in my head before talking about it. What are you doing for your birthday?''

''I have plans,'' she said regretfully.

He waited for an invitation to the party Anne had told him about, but it didn't come. What the hell. He'd crash it and stake his claim in front of all her friends. Maybe that would show her he might be exactly what she was looking for.

What did she want? What was she feeling?

Was she at all falling in love too—or had she just taken his fling suggestion seriously and used it as an excuse to act on the attraction between them? He frowned, trying to decipher it from her face.

It didn't work.

She smoothed the hair away from his forehead. ''You're serious this morning, Thomas.''

''I don't suppose I can convince you to stay in my bed for…a week or so?''

She kissed him softly. ''I'd love to. But I have to go. I have a lot to do before the guests arrive.''

''Can I help?''

''No, I'm fine. My friends are helping out. Well, my friends are doing everything. You know what Anne is like.''

''When do I see you again?'' He knew when. He was going to crash that party after all. But he was curious to see what she'd planned for them.

''I don't know…'' She hesitated. ''Maybe I could drop by when the party is over.''

''Sounds great. I'll give you a key.''

He'd give her a key? Okay, that settled it. He was a lost case.

She was looking at him quizzically, reading his mind. "You'll give me a key?"

"If you want. I mean, it's easiest that way." He shrugged. "Whatever."

"I'll just ring the doorbell, okay?"

"Okay," he said, strangely dissatisfied.

"What are you going to do today?"

He fiddled with her ear. It was as if he couldn't stop touching her. "Isn't it obvious? I'll be hunting down a birthday present for you."

"Really?" Her eyes lit up and sudden panic struck as he wondered where he would find something good enough for her. "You don't have to get me anything."

"I know I don't have to. I want to."

"When is your birthday?"

"Exactly five months away," he told her.

"Exactly?"

"Yes."

"So…it's your thirty-two and seven months birthday today. I'll get you something too."

She didn't expect to be around for his real birthday, did she? Thomas reluctantly let her pull away from him and get dressed. She didn't want him at her party either. But the hell with it. He'd crash it anyway. If little Danny was there, he'd charm him too, convince her he might even become responsible father material someday.

He grinned at her as she leaned down to kiss him goodbye.

He'd just had the perfect idea for a birthday present.

Lea sighed, fixing her hair in the bathroom, as she heard Anne run to the door, opening it to the first of her birthday guests.

It didn't feel right, after last night, to spend her birthday without Thomas. She'd wanted to invite him to the party, but it hadn't been possible. Not to his stepsister's house. He wouldn't have liked being put in a "boyfriend" role in front of a family member and she didn't want to watch him squirm out of the invitation.

He'd seemed disappointed that she hadn't asked him, though. Perhaps she should have told him why. Maybe she should call him and explain.

Don't be silly, Lea, she told herself. You're seeing him tonight. You can tell him then. She headed toward the living room, determined to have a great time tonight. There wouldn't be many guests, just a few friends.

And—she stopped short when she saw who was inside the living room—one uninvited one.

"How are things going with the dating thing?" Anne was asking Thomas.

"Fine."

"She won't tell me much about it. Has she met a lot of guys?"

Anne was out of sight, and Thomas's back was to her, but she saw him shrug. "A couple of guys."

"She's seeing someone special now, isn't she? I knew she was, a while ago. Paul something? Is that going anywhere?"

"I'm not chaperoning her dates anymore, Anne. Stop it. I'm not telling you what she doesn't want to tell you herself."

"Come on, Tom. Give me some details, please! I'm dying here. Just some tiny tidbit? She is seeing *someone*, isn't she? She won't even tell me that much."

Thomas sighed. "Yes, she's—sort of—seeing someone. I don't know if she wants it to work out, but I think he's the right guy for her.''

"Really? And this is Paul, right?''

"Anne, stop prying!''

"Sounds promising. Is she falling for him, do you think?''

"I don't know. Maybe. I hope so. I hope she realizes how right they are for each other.''

"You mean—they're in love?''

"I wouldn't go that far. I'm not sure she dares to fall in love. She keeps her emotions pretty much under lock and key until she feels safe. But things are progressing fine.''

"Wow. I didn't have a clue. Obviously I haven't interrogated her nearly enough.''

"Don't push it, Anne,'' Thomas said in a warning tone. "She wanted to find a husband. So far, it's going fine. Just leave her alone to sort through her feelings for the guy. The last thing she needs is more interference.''

Lea's heart pounded in her chest, pain increasing with every beat. They were talking about *Paul?*

She was falling for Paul? She wanted her husband to be *Paul?* Thomas was waiting for her to realize how right she and Paul were for each other?

Of course. She'd told Thomas all along what she wanted. Someone like Paul—not someone like him.

He was just her "last fling.'' It was all he'd ever wanted to be, all she'd told him he would be.

What she wanted to do was to yell that she'd never speak to either of them again and storm out, slamming the door hard behind her. But that would be too juvenile.

Instead she turned on her heel without a word, stormed into the kitchen, and slammed the door.

Men!

She whipped out her cell phone and stabbed in Paul's number, thankful that she hadn't removed it from the phone's memory already. If Thomas was insisting she was still dating Paul, then damn it, she would date Paul.

"Lea, what's wrong?"

She turned away from him. Paul's answering machine had finished its intro. "Hi, Paul, it's Lea…"

The phone was grabbed away from her. Thomas tossed it down on the counter, out of her reach. He cornered her off and grabbed her chin to forced her to look at him. She closed her eyes, knowing it was childish, but not caring. There was hurt in her eyes that she didn't want him to see and understand.

"Lea, what is that all about?"

His voice was angry and frustrated, and she opened her eyes to find the same in his eyes. "What's what all about?"

"Why are you calling Paul?"

"Why do you think I'm calling Paul? I thought I'd invite my fiancé to my thirtieth birthday party."

"Your *fiancé?*"

"Well, you practically announced my engagement to Paul in there, didn't you?"

"What are you talking about?"

Lea gritted her teeth and tried to move her head out of his grasp. She didn't succeed. "You were telling Anne my relationship with Paul was going fine. You were telling her all about how perfect we were for each other and how you couldn't wait for me to realize it.

Why shouldn't the *man of my dreams* come to my birthday party?''

Thomas released her chin, and put his hands on her shoulders instead, then moved them up to cradle her neck. He cursed, then took a deep breath and kissed her hard. "I wasn't talking about Paul, Lea. I was talking about me!"

His hands were warm. His lips were even warmer. She was warming up pretty rapidly herself. "What? But you said I didn't dare to love him!"

"Love who?"

"You! Paul!" A thirty-year-old woman shouldn't tear her hair out and shriek, should she? She tried to lower her voice, but it wasn't easy. She wasn't sure she was making much sense either, and she had the sinking feeling she might have—in a rather roundabout way—told Thomas she loved him. She pushed his arms away and took a step backward. "I don't know, whoever you were talking about."

Thomas touched her cheek for a moment, just with one finger, but it still burned through her entire body. "Lea, I was talking about *me*. I didn't know if you were ready to tell anyone about…us. I didn't want to give anything away to Anne until I'd talked to you. You didn't even want me at your birthday party. First I needed to see how you felt about me being here in the first place."

"I thought you wouldn't want to be there. You'd be labeled my boyfriend, and I didn't think you'd want that—"

"I do want to be your boyfriend. Why do you think I'm here?"

"You said…you'd be my fling."

"Lea…" He didn't touch her again, but she felt his

presence nevertheless. "How do you feel about long-term flings?"

She swallowed, trying to keep her voice from trembling. "Long-distance ones, too?"

"What?"

"Are you going to move to Japan?"

"No."

Silence. Her lungs had trouble working because there was just such intensity in his eyes.

He reached out, his fingers brushing her arm. "Lea, I have a present for you, out in the car. Will you wait for me while I go get it?"

She nodded, but he shook his head and took her hand. "I don't trust you. You're coming with me."

Midst all the confusion, she couldn't help but grin as he dragged her out of the house and to the car, where he lifted a big box out of the back seat.

"What's that?"

"You'll see." She was dragged back inside the house, and then out again when Thomas ran into Anne at the front door, staring at them with brows raised.

"Damn it. No privacy," he muttered, looking around. Then he started toward the garage door.

"Thomas, what are we doing in the garage?"

"Opening your present." He pulled the door open, turned the light on and closed the door behind them.

"Well," Lea said, wrinkling her noise against the smell of oil and dirt. "This is…cozy."

Thomas put the box on the floor and gestured at it. "Okay. You can open it now."

Lea looked at him suspiciously, but pulled at the bow, and opened the box. There was something inside, hidden in layers of bubble plastic and tissue paper. She lifted it carefully out and tore the plastic and paper away.

"What…is it?"

"What does it look like?"

"Well…it looks like what you'd call a horrible piece of art."

"Yes. I bought it with the check you gave me."

"You bought a horrible sculpture with that check?"

He smiled. "Yes. Just the way you like it, isn't it?"

She turned the sculpture, studying it. "You hate abstract art. Why did you buy it?"

"For you. Did you look at it?"

Lea took a second look. And a third one. "Yes. And?"

"What do you see?"

"A blob." She looked up, and saw he was waiting for a more in-depth answer. "Well, it's several blobs, clustered together."

"Exactly!"

"Am I missing something?"

"Don't you see the symbolism?"

"In the blobs?"

"Yes?"

She looked again. "Well…no."

Thomas sighed. "It's called *Family*."

"Oh," she whispered.

"You still want a husband and children, don't you?"

Her head shake was a surprise, even to herself. "I want you."

Thomas's hand encircled her wrist, and she put the sculpture carefully back into the box before allowing him to draw her close. "I bought it because I think I would like us to be a family."

"But you're not thirty-five yet. You don't want children until you're thirty-five and your life is over."

He grinned. "I'm getting there fast enough. A honeymoon, some serious time working on a baby, an entire pregnancy—hell, I might be thirty-five when it happens.''

Lea stared at him. ''You know what?''

''No.''

She shook her head ruefully. ''I believe it's a distinct possibility that I've fallen in love with you, you… wretched man.''

He laughed. ''Wretched man? Who taught you to curse?''

''It's not funny.'' She'd opened her heart and he just laughed at her language? She started squirming out of his arms, but he wouldn't let her.

''I'm falling right alongside you, Lea.''

That made her eyes, already filled with unshed tears, brim over.

''Okay. I get it. You didn't want to hear that.''

''I did. I do want to hear that. It's lovely, Thomas.''

''I love you, Lea.''

She was staring into his eyes and smiling, even as tears trickled down her cheeks. Generally he hated seeing women cry, but these tears were the most beautiful thing he'd ever seen. ''You finished falling?'' she asked, her voice hoarse. He reached out for her, pulling her close to him.

''Yeah. Last night. The red…whatever it was…did it.''

''How can you joke at a time like this?'' she asked, but the offended tone was kind of ruined by her uncontrollable giggles.

''I thought you'd be pleased to know that your purchase had the desired effect.''

''Yeah.'' She rested her head on his shoulder and snuggled into him. ''Want to have a baby in nine months?'' she mumbled into his jacket.

In *nine months?* He was ready—but he wasn't quite *that* ready. Thomas froze, then saw the wicked look in her eyes as she raised her head again. He pushed her against the wooden door and pinned her arms above her head. "You're teasing me, aren't you?"

"I would never do that, Tom."

"Liar. And we will have kids. But not right away, okay? I want you for myself for a little while first. I don't want a baby along on our honeymoon."

"Honeymoon? We're getting married?"

"Well, you *are* going to ask me, aren't you?"

"Am *I* going to ask *you*…" She squirmed against him, but his arms were tight around her. "Let me loose. I need to punch you."

"Wriggle all you want. I'm bigger and heavier, and besides, it just gives me ideas."

"I was just going to get down on one knee," she growled, still trying to break loose. "You know. Offer you a diamond ring. Let me go, and I'll show you."

"I love emancipated women."

She went still, brushed the hair out of her eyes and stared up at him, her eyes dark and intense. "Thomas, are you serious? About wanting a family?"

"Yeah. But it's a complicated process. It might take a while to get it right."

"You're right," Lea mused. "There are quite a lot of factors to take into account."

"We'll just keep practicing and see how it goes, okay?"

She smiled at him, a wicked sparkle in her eyes that told him it might be a while before they got back to that birthday party. "Perfect."

Do you like stories that get *up close* and *personal?*
Do you long to be loved *truly, madly, deeply...?*

If you're looking for emotionally intense, tantalizingly
tender love stories, stop searching and start reading

Harlequin Romance®

You'll find authors who'll leave you breathless, including:

Liz Fielding
Winner of the 2001 RITA Award for
Best Traditional Romance
(The Best Man and the Bridesmaid)

Day Leclaire
USA Today bestselling author

Leigh Michaels
Bestselling author with 30 million
copies of her books sold worldwide

Renee Roszel
USA Today bestselling author

Margaret Way
Australian star with 80 novels to her credit

Sophie Weston
A fresh British voice and a hot talent!

Don't miss their latest novels, coming soon!

HARLEQUIN®
Makes any time special®

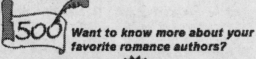

In *Changing Habits, New York Times* bestselling
author Debbie Macomber proves once again
why she's one of the world's most popular writers
of fiction for—and about—women.

DEBBIE MACOMBER

They were sisters once.

In a more innocent time, three girls enter the convent.
Angelina, Kathleen and Joanna come from very different
backgrounds, but they have one thing in common—
the desire to join a religious order.

Despite the seclusion of the convent house in Minneapolis,
they're not immune to what's happening around them, and
each sister faces an unexpected crisis of faith. Ultimately Angie,
Kathleen and Joanna all leave the sisterhood, abandoning the
convent for the exciting and confusing world outside. The
world of choices to be made, of risks to be taken. Of men
and romantic love. The world of ordinary women…

CHANGING HABITS

"Macomber offers a very human look at three women
who uproot their lives to follow their true destiny."
—*Booklist*

Available the first week of April 2004 wherever paperbacks are sold.

Harlequin Romance®

WHAT WOMEN WANT!
It could happen to you...

Every woman has dreams, deep desires, all-consuming passions or maybe just little everyday wishes!

In this miniseries from Harlequin Romance we're delighted to present a series of fresh, lively and compelling stories by some of our most popular authors—all exploring the truth about what women really want.

Don't miss the next book in this compelling miniseries:

May: *Rafael's Convenient Proposal* (#3795) by international bestselling author
Rebecca Winters

Mallory Ellis is facing the ultimate dilemma. Mediterranean aristocrat Rafael D'Afonso is offering her the family she's always wanted. But can she risk giving up her high-flying career for the chance of motherhood when all Rafael is offering is a marriage in name only...?

Available wherever Harlequin books are sold.

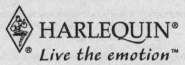

HARLEQUIN®
Live the emotion™

Visit us at www.eHarlequin.com

HRWWWRW

If you enjoyed what you just read,
then we've got an offer you can't resist!

Take 2 bestselling love stories FREE!

Plus get a FREE surprise gift!

Clip this page and mail it to Harlequin Reader Service®

IN U.S.A.
3010 Walden Ave.
P.O. Box 1867
Buffalo, N.Y. 14240-1867

IN CANADA
P.O. Box 609
Fort Erie, Ontario
L2A 5X3

YES! Please send me 2 free Harlequin Romance® novels and my free surprise gift. After receiving them, if I don't wish to receive anymore, I can return the shipping statement marked cancel. If I don't cancel, I will receive 6 brand-new novels every month, before they're available in stores! In the U.S.A., bill me at the bargain price of $3.34 plus 25¢ shipping & handling per book and applicable sales tax, if any*. In Canada, bill me at the bargain price of $3.80 plus 25¢ shipping & handling per book and applicable taxes**. That's the complete price and a savings of 10% off the cover prices—what a great deal! I understand that accepting the 2 free books and gift places me under no obligation ever to buy any books. I can always return a shipment and cancel at any time. Even if I never buy another book from Harlequin, the 2 free books and gift are mine to keep forever.

186 HDN DNTX
386 HDN DNTY

Name	(PLEASE PRINT)	
Address	Apt.#	
City	State/Prov.	Zip/Postal Code

* Terms and prices subject to change without notice. Sales tax applicable in N.Y.
** Canadian residents will be charged applicable provincial taxes and GST.
  All orders subject to approval. Offer limited to one per household and not valid to
  current Harlequin Romance® subscribers.
  ® are registered trademarks of Harlequin Enterprises Limited.

HROM02   ©2001 Harlequin Enterprises Limited

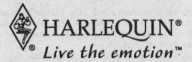

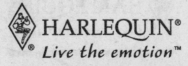